The Stupid Minivan

Or So It Seems…

The Stupid Minivan

and

More Tales
of
Midlife Madness

By Robb Lightfoot

Portions of the book have appeared
in The Funny Times
The Doggone Christmas List
and
aNewsCafe

An eBook version of this collection is available at
major retail outlets.

You may contact the publisher or the author at:

Or So It Seems Publishing
PO Box 214
Palo Cedro, CA 96073
robb@orsoitseems.com

ISBN: 0988785420
ISBN-13: 978-0-9887854-2-7

DEDICATION

I dedicate this book with love, respect and gratitude to Karin, my wife and best friend of over 30 years. Thanks for your support and encouragement when I wanted to quit. Our life and journeys together have been the real reward. Thanks, too, to our four children, Amanda, Nicole, Rebecca and Joe, for letting me to tell these tales—and not disowning me.

CONTENTS

DEDICATION…………………………….....v

ACKNOWLEDGMENTS…………………..ix

Food Follies – EXPIRED……………………1

Going Batty…………………………………..7

Play by the
Rules…………………………………...………14

Tall Tales and Tedious Trips……………….....21

The SMV - Stupid
Minivan………………………………………..26

Miss Directions……………………………....36

How To Root For Your Olympic Hero……..43

Sleeping With Darth Vader…………………56

Lawn Care for the Horticulturally Impaired…61

What the Tooth Fairy Won't Tell You………68

The Garbage Man Cometh…………………..73

Toying With Trouble………………………...81

Cell Mates……………………………………...86

The World's Worst Movie…………………..90

Minimal Effort Voting -
A Public Service Announcement…………....98

Lost and Found…………………………104

Halloween Pointers..............................111

The Doggone Christmas List..................117

Better Fussing in Five Minutes a Day.........121

Letters to Santa..................................127

National Fruitcake Month -

A Mayan Warning...............................135

Down with Christmas Trees...................142

Lucy-the-Dog's Resolutions...................148

About The Author.............................154

ACKNOWLEDGMENTS

First and foremost, my deepest gratitude goes out to my writing buddies—Charlie Price, Melinda Kashuba, Kathryn Gessner, Jim Dowling and Carla Jackson. I am indebted to you for your sage advice and for sharing my joys and sorrows.

Amanda Lightfoot-Wright's sharp-eyed copyediting improved this manuscript immensely. Thank you for your patience and professionalism.

A tip of the hat to Doni Chamberlain who gave me space in her publication aNewsCafe and the freedom to try my hand at a variety of humor forms. Your willingness to let me wander around the creative landscape was vital to my growth.

To the dozens of English, journalism and creative writing and comedy instructors who guided me, you have enriched my life more than I can say.

My former editor Mike Stepanovich of the Bakersfield Californian taught and encouraged me during my early years as professional writer. He remains a trusted mentor and friend.

Finally, a nod to a gifted teacher and author—Tony D'Souza. Tony, I'd been struggling in isolation for years, and you gave me the key I'd been lacking. You said in one of your presentations that "no one does it alone." A simple but profound truth that allowed me to reach out. Your class also was the genesis of my writing group. We all owe you.

This book exists because of all these true friends and my family.

Palo Cedro, CA, December 2012

*The Stupid Minivan
and
More Tales
of Midlife Madness*

FOOD FOLLIES –
EXPIRED

"Hey Dad. You gonna pack the potato salad?" My son pointed to a container on the kitchen counter. "It's been out all night."

I was the foreman on that day's lunch-assembly-line. We were behind schedule, and I wasn't looking for quality control.

"Probably."

1

"But it's got mayo?" He frowned.

"Yep."

"And mayo's made with eggs?" His voice trailed off.

"Right again." I said.

"Mr. Harvick, my life-skills teacher, says bad eggs make you sick."

"No problem." I winked. "These eggs graduated top of their class."

My son chewed on his lip. "I'll pass on the potatoes."

"Really, son? Who you going to believe? Him or me?"

"Well…."

I was crushed. It was one of those moments when you know that you're no longer the source-of-all-wisdom for your child.

"Tell you what. I'll bet you $5 it's OK."

"Five bucks?" My son's interest was revived

"I'm eating it. And if I don't die, you owe me a fiver."

"But if you croak, how do I collect?"

I guess they don't teach compassion in life-skills.

But, *really*, how much should you worry about food safety? I'm living proof that the immune system is a thing of wonder. On the other hand, my wife, a nurse, is pretty careful. She throws things out that look *perfectly fine*. Just because they have *"expired."* In addition to the potato salad, I'm making myself a ham sandwich, and I offer her one.

"What's the date?" She asks.

I glance at my watch. "It's the 5th."

"NO. THE EXPIRATION DATE."

"Oh, I don't know." I looked at the torn wrapper and didn't see it.

"The ham's from the last Costco run," she says.

"If you say so."

"That was weeks ago." She shakes her head. "You really want food poisoning?"

I eyed my sandwich. It looks harmless enough.

"Sam-I-Am ate ham that was green and lived," I said.

"Did you ever see him in a sequel?"

"Well… no," I admitted. So I turned the wrapper inside out, and found the magic numbers. "Looks like it's dated… yesterday."

"Is that the sell-by date or the use-by date?" she asked.

"Don't know."

"Then I wouldn't eat it," she warned.

"But it's yesterday. One day's growth is gonna kill me?"

"If it got left out…"

"It didn't," I said. But I couldn't be sure, not without watching the surveillance tapes. Maybe it had broken parole and made off with the mozzarella. My wife had planted the seed of doubt. So I went back to the fridge, the land of suspicious lunch meat, seeing if we had something else. "We've got some sliced chicken, fresh in the wrapper."

"Fresh? I don't remember buying it," she said.

"I think I did."

"Expiration?" she asked.

I looked on the wrapper. "Best by … last Tuesday."

"No thanks."

"Hey, it's unopened. No one left it out."

"It should have been used weeks ago."

"'Best by...' doesn't mean it will be bad."

"Mystery meat." She wrinkled her nose.

"It's chicken, not cafeteria food."

"No. Thank. You."

"I'll eat it."

"Then I'll visit you in the ER." She sighed, "Look. I can make my own sandwich."

"No," I said. "It's my turn and I'll do it."

"OK. Then just make me a peanut butter sandwich, please." She cocked her head. "And you have washed your hands.... Right?"

So I dug around in the cupboard and found a dusty peanut butter jar and a squeeze container of granulated honey. I waved them in her face. "This is what you want?"

5

"Please."

"But this stuff has been in there since Y2K." I said.

"It keeps."

"OK," I shrugged. "Dessert?"

"Maybe. What do we have?"

I checked the fridge, freezer and cookie jar. Nothing. Our daughter had cleaned out the fresh fruit.

I dug deep into the pantry, exploring shelves that I didn't know we had. There, hidden and forgotten, I found a relic of bygone era—an ancient package of Twinkies.

"Ooooh." I smiled, and tucked the treat in her lunch. "I found something special just for you."

"Thanks."

I handed her the bag.

"You'll like it." I kissed her on the cheek. "Doesn't expire until the year 2525."

GOING BATTY

Rebecca saw it first, clinging on the wall. "Eeeuuuuwwww. Is it a bat?" She pointed to an object that looked like a wad of chewing gum covered with fur.

I squinted, and stepped forward for a better view. We both stood outside the Butte County government building, staring. Just then, a uniform-wearing-person walked by, and we pointed to the "thing on the wall." Turns out, this was an actual-government-employee.

"What's that?" I asked.

"Beats me," came the definitive answer. So, she took a picture of the creature, and emailed it to animal control.

Gawker number four stopped while we were waiting on a ruling from the judges.

"Kind of small to be a bat," the passer-by said. As we waited, Butte County's best, experts in the field of USOs, unidentified stationary objects, poured over the image, checked their databases, and probably looked it up on Wikipedia. Almost instantly, they called back.

"Yup. It's a bat," the actual-government-employee said.

"So what now?" I asked.

"Nothing," she shrugged. "They said to just leave it alone."

Now this just seemed wrong to me. After all, the age-old instinct of guys everywhere is to stomp on disgusting things. I, myself, had participated in an attempted bat stomping incident years ago while saving the lives of a trailer full of small children and my wife.

It all began so innocently. It was a typical, 112 degree summer morning in Redding. One of those days when everyone has two questions on their minds. First, why do I live here and second, where can I find a camping space on the coast? Since we couldn't answer either question, we set out on a quest, packing up our four kids, plus one-more-for-ballast, in the mini-van. We hitched up the tent-trailer and went west—destination Patrick's Point. This is a place known for its rugged beauty, fog-shrouded trees, and oodles and gobs of "natural wild stuff," like elk, humongous bugs, and banana slugs.

Our kids were determined to find a banana slug. My wife, Karin, and I thought it would be a harmless distraction while we fixed lunch. Amanda, our oldest, quickly nabbed a slug and then passed it around. This provided a science-based learning opportunity for everyone. The kids learned that the reason the slugs are yellow is, apparently, that they are mostly snot. Excuse me, the scientific term is mucus. Karin and I learned that this stuff goes well beyond anything you've ever found in the nastiest of handkerchiefs. We spent the better part of an hour and an entire bottle of Dawn trying to clean the kids' hands so that they could touch food and not have it slide through their fingers.

The rest of the afternoon was full of standard-issue costal stuff, mainly going down to the beach, carefully selecting souvenirs and filling five buckets, one per kid, of pretty sea shells and special stones that weighed only slightly more than a VW Beetle. Then, because the kiddos were tired, the adults got to lug all these treasures up, waaaay up the cliff, to the car. Through the magic of heat and evaporation, we found just a short while later, that the contents had dried out and turned into ordinary rocks and stinky stuff that required ventilating the van. We ended the day with a small fire, the traditional toasted marshmallows and camp songs. Contented, we finally tucked ourselves in for the evening.

The first screams came at 2 am. My wife, a nurse, was hiding under her pillow, yelling "A bat! A bat! A bat!" I stood bolt upright, banged my head on a pipe, and then flopped down on top of her. I crawled to the door to chase it out.

"NO! NO! NO!"

"What?" I shouted back. By then, all the kids were yelling, too.

"Get it! Get it! Get it!" she commanded.

"WHY IN THE SAM HILL?"

My wife and I have different memories of the event at this point. She said that she calmly explained the "risks of exposure." Namely, that there's the distinct possibility of getting rabies when you wake up having "shared sleeping space" with a bat, and

10

it needs to be tested. Otherwise, everyone must get "prophylactic treatment." This is not what it sounds like.

But what I clearly remember was the line, "IT'S $2,000 FOR EACH OF US IF YOU DON'T CATCH IT!"

I may have been half asleep, but I could still multiply... 7 x ... "OH MY GOD..." Now *I* began screaming, thrashing, and stomping around in the dark looking for something, anything, inside the trailer to use. I found a fishing net, with mesh big enough for tennis balls to pass through. But it was all I had, and I whipped it about until I caught the bat.

It crawled out.

So, I thrashed around again, and again. Ten minutes of catch and release, until the exhausted little creature could not get free and we trapped it in a Maxwell coffee can.

The next day, bleary-eyed, we packed up and headed to the Humboldt County Health Department. On our way out of the park, my pathologically-honest wife told the ranger we were removing a bit of wildlife— the bat.

"You can't do that," the ranger said, explaining that she was president of the "Friends of the Bat Society" and it was her expressed intent to protect all bats, including little "Maxwell."

"It could have rabies," my wife said.

"Most bats don't carry disease."

"It's got to be tested, or we'll have to get treatment."

"They kill the bat to do that, you know." The ranger scowled.

"Sorry, but we have to know."

"You can't leave," the ranger said, crossing her arms and taking a step towards the front of the van.

"Watch us," my wife said.

I hit the gas.

Now it turns out the bat wasn't rabid, but the sad fact is they have to yank out the brain to know for sure. And when it comes down to the big moment of truth, the bat or my family, on most days I'll go with my family.

I flashed back on this as I stood outside the Butte County building, feeling instinctive, deep-in-the-gut anti-bat urges. But I knew, intellectually, of course, that little-bitty Maxwell the 2nd shouldn't be stomped. So I let him be. After all, I didn't have a net, an actual government-employee-in-uniform was telling me to just leave it alone, and my wife wasn't there hiding under a pillow to cheer me on.

PLAY BY THE RULES

Grandma was always packin,' and rarin' to go. She carried her own dice, and could, on occasion, shoot them straight and true. But usually they took an odd bounce. 'Bama couldn't help it. It was her '*Yahtzee* elbow.'

"Hey, 'Bama, that's cheating," my brother whined.

14

"No, hon, they just up and jumped on my arm," Grandma smiled.

"But you bumped them after they'd stopped."

"Did I? Well hush my mouth." Her eyes opened wide. "If you like, I could roll again."

So she did. A couple tumbled off the table. She grabbed both in mid-air, and held them up for us to see.

"Two sixes."

Mom cocked her head. "Really?"

"They were gonna be sixes."

Mom rolled her eyes. "Well you should work for the FBI."

"Maybe I do."

"Then arrest yourself, scofflaw."

Grandma winked, and penciled in a zero. "Ah… Just funnin' ya."

And fun she was. 'Bama had more trick shots than Minnesota Fats.

Yahtzee wasn't our family's only passion. We also were Monopolists, members of a cult that deprives you of sleep, strips your

15

wealth, and lands you in jail. Once hooked, you're forced to find fresh recruits. It's not easy. I lost a few friends by confining them in a small room, spending hours on end passing 'Go,' until we fell into a stupor.

So usually it was just me and my brother, JD. Since I was older, and more "responsible," I got to be the banker. Having your hands on other people's money is the best part of the game. Once, I wanted to buy hotels but was short on cash. I hit upon a creative financing scheme that would impress Goldman-Sacs.

"How about the bank loans us both $5,000?"

"Why?" JD frowned.

"For… improvements."

"Hotels on Boardwalk? Right?'

"Could be." I said.

JD scowled. "And I'll land on them."

"But you'll have $5,000."

"Until I lose it."

"Yeah. Then I can pay the bank back, and you'll go bankrupt."

"That stinks." JD said.

16

"It's business, little brother, and I'm gonna take the cash, even if you don't."

"Better not!"

"Show me where it says I can't!" I waved the rule book in his face.

"I'm tellin'."

Mom was summoned. She scanned the instructions.

"Nope. Not allowed."

"Ah, Mom. You can divvy stuff up for a shorter game."

"At the start," Mom sighed. "You don't change rules halfway through."

"But they're *nice hotels*," I said. "It's progress."

Mom shook her head. "Playing by the rules builds character. Try it, you'll see." She left, and my brother flashed a grin.

"Told ya'," JD said.

"OK." I put the rule book at my side. "She said I had to play *by* them, not *with* them. Now, how about some cash?"

"MOM!"

⁎⁎

Yet Mom did have a point. Playing by the rules does offer many valuable lessons. *Life*, for example, lets you taste the sweetness of "revenge" and sample the sin of gambling. It's all there in the rule book. Sure, *Life* touts college and a career, but you can place side-bets and spin the wheel. It's a great way to end up in the poor house.

Games teach us about emotions, too. Take *Sorry*. I learned how to pulverize my kid sister and see her dissolve in tears. Then I had to comfort her and tell her I was *sorry* she'd lost. Really, though, I was *thrilled* I'd won. At age 12, winning was *it*. As my baseball coach said: "Show me a good loser, and I'll show you a loser."

I did embrace one lesson from "Life" I decided to attend college. There, Backgammon was the game of choice. I played it to decompress during study breaks. Then came marriage, graduation, and kids. Old, familiar board games from my childhood crept back into my life along with our little rug rats - *Candyland*, *Chutes and Ladders*, even *Sorry* .... But the fun began for real when the kiddos were old enough to play my favorite, *Scrabble*. It was a big moment. We divided up the tiles, and I laid down my first word in family competition.

"What's a 'snarfz,' Daddy?" my daughter asked.

"It's a rodent that lives in Namibia." I smiled and pointed towards our *World Books*. "You should look it up."

Across the table, my wife cleared her throat. "Really?"

"Oh, all right." I shrugged, taking the tiles, and losing my turn. "Maybe there are snarfzs and we just haven't discovered them."

"We'll leave that to Dr Seuss." She then took her turn, laying down "fabric" next to "ate."

"Fabricate," she smiled, patting me on the arm. "Triple word... double letter... 52 points."

"Slick," I said.

"And by the book."

Yes, rulebooks and reason still reside with Mothers, Inc. But you can't fight genetics. Case in point. My son and his older sisters were playing hide-and-seek when the four of them piled into the kitchen.

"Joe's cheating," the girls said in three-part harmony. "He's tagged out, but he won't be 'it.'"

19

Joe shrugged. "No I'm not."

"Yeah-huh," the girls said.

"I was touching the tree." To prove his point, he held up a twig.

"I think they meant the trunk." I hid a smile.

"But they didn't *say* that."

Karin looked at me and shook her head. "That acorn didn't fall far from the tree."

"We don't want to play hide-and-seek with *him* anymore." The girls pouted. "We want a game with *real* rules."

"OK, OK." I nodded and pointed at the table. "How about some Yahtzee?"

TALL TALES AND TEDIOUS TRIPS

I come from a family that loves good stories. When I was a kid, at our dinner table, everyone talked about their day, usually all at the same time. We'd take turns topping one another. There was lots of love, some shouting, laughter, and many a memorable tale. *Some* of the stories even had the added advantage of being true. Dinner guests who were first-time visitors were often taken aback until they learned to just wade in and speak their piece.

At grade school, I would talk up a storm, retelling these stories, shouting out answers to the teachers' questions, and filling in the punch lines to other people's jokes. I wanted attention, and I got attention. Lots of attention. I was given my own special reserved-seating desk in the principal's office. As I recall, my first-grade teacher had a stack of referral slips with my name already dittoed on them, and the box "talking in class" checked off. I remember this, and it may have actually happened....

So I survived school and, oddly enough, ended up back in the classroom again. I make my living by forcing other people to talk in class—I'm a speech teacher. My subjects include how to overcome fear of talking—hint, do it a lot—and factual research methods. In fact, I'm all for facts. But I also cover literature in performance, and storytelling, too. I know that a good story sometimes wanders into the land of the tall tale.

Great fiction reveals the truth by telling a compelling story. But even non-fiction narrative can offer conflicting views of reality. It just depends. My graduate thesis was a study of "competing political narratives," which is a fancy way of saying I examined two stories where the heroes and villains were reversed and each side wanted to win to gain a big hunk of real estate. Who or what to believe? It's hard to know sometimes.

When my four kids were little, we'd pass the time on long trips by telling original, convoluted stories. It worked like this. My wife, Karin, or I would begin the yarn, and after a few paragraphs—a chapter—hand it off to one of the kids. The new narrator would pick up the thread and go on. The story would unravel as it moved around the van. By the time it made it back to me, the plot was a hopeless tangle. How? Why? Who knew?

Sometimes, when we were overdue for a rest stop, a back-seat troll might kill off my favorite character. One time this happened, just as the story-telling-staff was passed back to me, and I decided a case of literary CPR was in order. I revived my character, Wilbur.

A howl arose from the back seat.

"You can't do that," the Greek chorus said.

"Do what?" I replied in innocence.

"Bring back Wilbur."

"But he's not really dead."

"They found his body floating in the lake," my daughter Amanda said.

"Or so it seemed," I said. "Later tests proved it wasn't him."

My daughter fumed. "So who was it?"

"Don't know." Somehow, this answer didn't satisfy Amanda, She'd taken a personal dislike to Wilbur. All my heroes were named Wilbur, and she'd apparently had enough of them.

So when the story circled back around to her, she sought her own revenge. Wilbur was about to get married... a happy ending was in view. And then Amanda struck.

"But the police arrested Wilbur and threw him in jail. He was convicted of murder and executed."

"Hey," I protested, "Why would they do that?"

"Because it was someone impersonating Wilbur," she said.

"But the tests proved it wasn't."

"Or so it seemed," she said. I saw her smile in my rear-view mirror. "But the Wilbur-impersonator snuck into the lab and changed the test tubes."

"How did they know?"

"He left a fingerprint on the test tube, and a brilliant investigator named Amanda figured it out," she said. "The end."

And that was when the "Or So It Seems" method of storytelling entered our family history. At least that's how I remember it. It could have happened. Or not.

You'll have to ask Amanda.

THE SMV - STUPID MINIVAN

"You are what you repeatedly drive."

Aristotle

"You don't have to do this," Karin said. She held her keys out, and I gave her mine.

"It's my turn, I guess."

"OK, but I know you don't like my van."

That was putting it mildly. I hated everything about her Windstar—The SMV – The Stupid Minivan.

It was huge. It was ugly. It had the optional peanut-butter-stained interior with a pungent not-new-car smell. The carpeting contained the historical record of our four kids, captured in layers of beach sand, smashed bananas, and melted ice cream, all well-preserved by a protective coating of dog hair.

Of course it hadn't always been that way. Only a few years before, Karin had decided it was time to ditch our "classic car," a Chevy 9-passenger wagon, and get a box-on-wheels minivan.

We did research, finding Fords the safest and most reliable. By and by we were at the used car lot, standing next to a putrid-green, recycled Windstar.

Several salesmen circled, smelling fresh meat. One finally dove on us for the kill.

"Great choice," he smiled. Karin nodded. I studied my shoelaces. "Let's disable the alarm so you can look inside."

I blinked. "People *steal* these things?"

The salesman was unfazed. "Do we need to talk financing?"

I rolled my eyes.

"Can you give us a quote?" Karin said. "Just for fun."

The salesman scribbled a price on a piece of paper and handed it to me.

"Is this the serial number?" I asked.

"It's a great deal."

"For you." I studied the amount. It was more than my parents had paid for their home. "Is this in American dollars or Chuck E. Cheese coupons?"

"Robb…" Karin whispered. "Don't be rude."

The salesman smiled. I didn't.

I started to walk away. Karin didn't.

"Do we *need* this stupid minivan?" I groaned.

"You saw the Chevy's safety numbers. What do you think?"

I looked at our kids in the rearward-facing seat, and I flinched. Our wagon had the crashworthiness of a cardboard box. "Well…."

Karin smiled. "You'll be glad."

"Dual air bags," the salesman cawed.

"Oh… yeah," I sighed.

"I'll throw in a tank of gas."

"OK. OK." I threw up my hands, the customary move in a hold-up.

By dinnertime, the Chevy was gone and the SMV sat in our driveway. Karin was thrilled. She had a safe and almost-new Mommobile. I consoled myself that since I still had my pickup, I didn't have to drive that green toad. And for the most part, I didn't.

Time passed. The kids grew, and Karin returned to work. Her hours increased. I adjusted my schedule to cover afternoons, taking over the shuttle service. This included music lessons, dance lessons, soccer practice, doctor's visits, and a zillion after-school activities. And it meant that I drove the van.

A lot.

We'd trade keys, but every afternoon had *some* event that required me to drive the SMV. So… one fateful day I took Karin's keys for good. She drove off the next morning in the pickup. But it was, in theory, still *my truck*.

I was in minivan denial for a long time. I wore sunglasses and a hat, drove the back roads, sought out the vacant corners of parking lots. It didn't work.

"See you've got a minivan," a coworker chuckled. "Won't catch me driving one of those things."

"It's my wife's," I explained. "I'm just running some errands."

He smiled. "About two months' worth, I'd say."

Why can't people just mind their own business? I'd have attracted less attention if I'd ridden through town on a bicycle, buck-naked.

My brain clung to a pickup-guy fantasy. But then disaster struck – my truck scrambled an engine. Now I may be from Bakersfield, but dead trucks are *not* driveway ornaments. So it had to go. The question was: What should replace it?

A tough choice. Where I came from, real men drove pickups. I learned to drive in my Dad's Chevy step side at age eight. My first truck was an El Camino. My heart said "buy a safer car for Karin to drive." My reptilian brain stem wanted a pickup.

I moped. Karin tried to cheer me up.

"You know, the van can haul just about anything," she said.

"Can it haul manure?"

"You need a truckload of manure?"

"Could be," I said. "Or maybe a ton of gravel."

"Axner Landscaping delivers."

"Yeah, right."

"Anything else?" Karin asked. "Should we buy a pickup?"

I sighed. "No. They're not safe. I don't want you getting hurt."

She hugged me. "You're a good man."

Pickup gone, I focused on the business at hand, getting everyone to the right place at the right time. Gradually my disappointment eased as the van routinely took me to work and the kids to play. It delivered us safely into and out of many adventures. It made runs with petulant pooches, caged-and-enraged cats and even the occasional fish tank or freaked-out cockatiel. As far as I know there's still a gerbil somewhere in the center console. And on some somber occasions, it dutifully ushered ailing pets to their final vet visit.

The van saw us through big life changes. Packed, stacked and dangling bicycles, it bore our two oldest children off to college and us through a move to a smaller home.

In the space of six years, we put more than 160,000 miles on the Windstar. I knew it so well I could parallel park it in one shot in the worst traffic. I made my peace with it. I even admitted that it could haul almost anything the truck could, and in the rain, no less.

But the big moment in attitude-adjustment came when I learned how to brag on it with other man-vanners – driving Dads who cover the soccer shift. I knew I was a member of this fraternity when some dude first challenged my van.

"So how many cup holders do you have?"

"Three," I said.

"That's all? Ha!"

I smiled wanly. He kept at it.

"Built-in DVD player?"

I ignored him.

"Surround sound?" he smirked.

"Ah, no," I admitted.

He gloated. But I was ticked. I looked over and saw his little van, one of those sawed-off jobs with a lame four-banger.

"OK, man. Let's talk cargo capacity," I said. He looked uneasy. "I've got the extend version." I gave him a wink. "How big's yours?"

That shut him up.

So I managed the man-van thing. Yeah, the Windstar was still ugly but rock-solid reliable. I grew to respect it as I watched the years and odometer roll by. We saw 170k and 180k pass with no major problems. Impressive.

But then an urgent family matter caused us to drive more than 10,000 miles in two months. We hit 190k, 195k, and she began showing her age. The electronics got dicey. The windows stuck down in a thunderstorm. The wipers acted up. Gauges took the day off. Irksome, but the van kept going. The bigger worry... a strange gurgling sound and a radiator that kept going dry. Yet it didn't leak.

It needed work, but money was tight. So I kept adding coolant, hoping for the best. Finally, at 203,000 miles, I took it in to be smogged. I guessed the heater core was gone, but the diagnosis was terminal – a blown head gasket.

"You went HOW FAR with this leak?" my mechanic asked. And I told him. "Amazing," he shook his head. "Your engine can seize within 100 miles when this happens."

We did the math on repairs. "Time to put her down," I was told. I stuck a notice on

Craigslist, and within a day a salvage-buyer came.

"Is this the junker?" He pointed at the Windstar.

"It's *my van*," I said, annoyed.

He paid me, and I handed the keys over. Then the salvage guy started the engine, and drove up on his trailer. It was an odd moment. After years of complaining, I was now a van-free man. I watched him strap it down. It looked tired, but still willing.

Yeah, it was beat. The electronics were shot, the engine was blown, and the interior was threadbare. But just like the skin horse in the Velveteen Rabbit, its stains made it shabby ... and beautiful. I watched the trailer pull away, our old van bouncing out of sight, thus ending our long journey together.

So I got my wish, and I'm back in something smaller, cheaper, and less un-cool. But Karin was right. I'm glad we bought that ugly, oversized box. And the thing is... I miss it. I really do.

Stupid minivan.

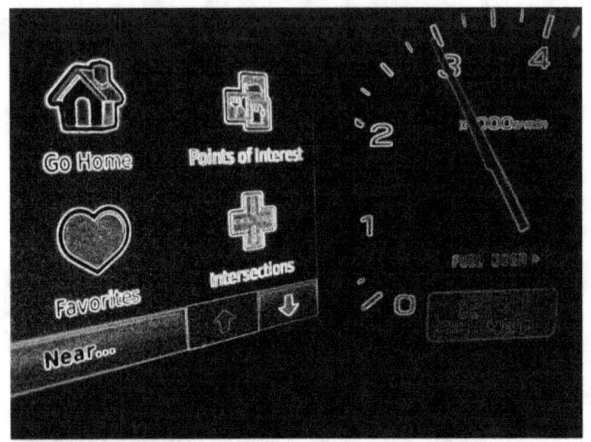

MISS DIRECTIONS

Since the days when cavemen had to get to the convenience store without crossing the tar pits, we've all had to either give or receive directions. It's a skill, like kissing and telling jokes, that everyone *thinks* they do well.

My wife can both find our way here, there, and back again without pinning a note to our shirts, but when it comes to *giving* directions, we speak different languages.

She's a minimalist, a code-talker. Her directions are brief and to the point, and work best if you already know how to get where you're going. Karin disagrees, of course, but

36

I've seen her written directions, given to friends, on how to find our home.

"Turn left by the old Jacques' place, drive until you pass the barn that used to be red, count to ten, and then go south."

The problem is, of course, that the Jacques no longer live there. The mailbox now says "Anderson." The barn that was once red comes after a barn that IS red, and it's not possible to turn south off the main road, well not EXACTLY south. When appraised of this, she'll clarify, "South-ish, maybe."

People who get my wife's directions find them easy to commit to memory. This is a good thing because you may well be driving a long, looooong time before you find our home. A recent report by the National Highway Traffic Safety Administration discovered that crop circles in our town are caused by people driving around and around after turning south off the main highway.

My approach, the guy-way, is to give super-detailed directions, complete with historical references, restaurant reviews, brief memoires of our family story, such as who got sick at a particular turn, and other exciting details. People who have trouble sleeping at night can reread these directions and nod right off.

I've also been told that after reading my directions, many people decide that they'd be better off staying home and inviting my wife over.

So there's a competitive element to direction-giving. After my wife gives her directions, I give mine. When the hapless guests finally arrive, I'll ask: "Which set was best?" The wise ones would look at Karin, then at me, and say both directions, taken together—like a combination drug therapy—worked just perfectly.

These days, though, the most common answer is: "Oh, we didn't need them. We just used the GPS."

Sad to say, this is a dying art. And we're helping to kill it — we finally broke down and bought a GPS. It's put a whole new thrill to driving. I just punch in the address, press a button, and Lizzie-from-London tells me how to get there.

"In .5 miles, turn right on Old Alturas," the clipped British accent says. I'm about to make the turn, when a very familiar American voice countermands the direction.

"I wouldn't go that way," Karin says.

"Why not?" I ask.

"Rebecca's ex-boyfriend lives down there, and he'll think you're checking up on him."

I have to decide in a flash which of the two women I'll obey.

I drive past the turn.

"Recalculating." Lizzie says, sounding annoyed. "Turn right in .4 miles on Irene."

"Nope," my wife says.

"Why?" I venture.

"Don't ask," she says with finality.

The funny thing is, after years of married life, this really constitutes an explanation, or as much of one as you're likely to get.

So, we go on past turn after turn, irritating "Miss Directions," as my wife has come to call the other woman who shares the intimate space of the front seat. Eventually, all three of us arrived at our destination the same way that airlines do, taking the "Great Circle" route that sends you over the polar ice cap.

This wasn't the first time that Karin had taken exception to my electronic playmate. A couple of summers ago I was making my way through a strange town, squinting at the glowing GPS map and hanging on Lizzie's every word. But something was amiss. Every time I turned, Lizzie had second thoughts, "recalculated," and then told me do go back the way I came. I was going around in my own Great Circle, as the minutes ticked away and we got closer and closer to missing our appointment. All the while, Karin was telling me a story about one of her students, or the kids, or her dogs, I think. I really couldn't tell you since I was in the Traffic Twilight Zone, where there is NO DIRECT ROAD to your goal, sort of like driving in Vermont.

Karin took command, breaking my trance, when she reached over and turned the GPS off.

"Really?" she said. "You've gone around this block three times already. You never ask me to navigate anymore." Karin unfolded a dusty map. "Need help?"

"Yeah, turn Lizzie back on." I had pulled over, afraid to miss another turn.

"Look, I've been finding our way for more than 20 years. I'll get you there."

"I don't want to be late," I said, reaching for the GPS myself. Karin held it out of my reach, giving me a look that said "Is it her or me?"

"OK," I threw my hands up. "I don't know how to get there." I glanced at my watch. I'd allowed 10 minutes of "wiggle room," and I wasn't sure when my next turn was. Karin studied her road atlas.

"You'll turn up here, on the right," and she waved vaguely in a southeasterly direction. I pulled back on the road.

"How far?"

"Just a bit," she said.

"A bit, or a little bit?"

"Can't tell yet, but I'll let you know." She held the atlas out at arm's length, adjusted her glasses, and then slowly, when she thought I wasn't looking, turned the map right side up.

"It might be faster to turn left," she said.

"Where?"

"Back there," she said, smiled, and hid her face behind the map a bit. "Oops."

"Are you recalculating?" I asked.

"Not at all," she said. "I know exactly where I am."

"And that would be?"

41

"Sitting next to the guy who's has a decision to make."

"And that would be?"

She smiled. "Whether he wants to sleep tonight with me... or Miss Directions."

Lizzie wound up in the glove box, and we ended up, eventually, within walking distance of our destination a good 10 minutes sooner than Lizzie would have gotten us there.

At least by Karin's calculations.

And I'm not arguing with that.

An error occurred. Please try again later.

HOW TO ROOT FOR YOUR OLYMPIC HERO

In 92 Not-So-Easy Steps

A Special Report – LONDON 2012

Much as I wish I could have gone to London, I'm here at home watching TV with my DVR digital recorder. But, of all the sports, there's one that simply must be watched live—our own hometown gal, Megan Rapinoe playing for the gold.

Here's how it's done.

Step 1 – Forget when the game begins. Be doing something else that's complicated, demands your total attention and which is hard to put aside.

Step 2 – Have your wife remind you that the game begins in just minutes.

Step 3 – Frantically finish complicated project while wife turns on big screen TV, tunes to the Old Peacock Network--channel 248.

Steps 4-92 are spelled out as they coincide with game-time, or GT.

-4 Minutes Before GT – Hear wife say, "It's not working," waving the TV remote about, simultaneously looking at her smart phone's tiny screen.

-3:30 – Wife, talking to the TV, says "THE TEAMS ARE ON THE FIELD!"

-3:15 – Four remotes in hand, wife fails to tune to Olympics.

-3 – You, also known as Home Tech Support, spring into action, and grab the remote, pressing buttons 2-4-8.

-2:45 – Wife glares at you. "I DID THAT already." You both stare at the "Info Screen" on channel 251, plugging the Old

Peacock Network. No soccer players are visible on screen.

-2:40 – Home Tech Support has flash of insight. "Must be pay-for-view."

-2:30 – "You sure?"

-2:25– "Pretty sure."

-2:15 – "But the Old Peacock website says you can watch it live on the web," wife says with lower lip protruding.

-2:10 – Wife grabs her laptop, brings up Olympic News, displaying the Road-Kill Bird logo and randomly clicks about the page. Nothing happens.

-1:30 – Wife looks at cell phone, still clutching and clicking her laptop.

GAMETIME – Wife stands, dashes into your office, thrusts uncooperative computer into your hands, retreats to corner with phone.

+:15 Seconds – You scroll down, and see a link to live viewing. You click link.

+:25 – "The Saucer Network" – Online Login Screen appears.

+:30 – You realize while you have a "Saucer" account, you don't have a "Saucer ONLINE Account."

+:35 – You find the link "How To Create An Online Account."

+:40 – Screen appears asking for *10-digit serial number* off the back of satellite receiver.

+:55 – You remove from cabinet, yanking several cables loose and say magic tech-incantation %$**##!

+1:00 – Wife asks you if "everything is OK?"

+1:15 – You find several stickers, but no 10-digit number.

+1:20-3:59 – Reattach %$**## cables.

+4:00 – Return to wife's laptop. See that "Option B" allows you to enter a *16-digit Saucer account number.*

+4:05-6:59 – Go out to garage. Root through old boxes of paper, looking for an antique "Saucer" bill back in the days before you went paperless.

+7:00 – Fail to find bill. Find instead cool Grateful Dead album. Decide to call 2-Tin-Cans-&-A-String phone company. They bundle your phone, net, satellite, and pizza-delivery service.

+7:01-7:45 – Look for phone book. Find *old* phone book, fail to find number. Deride ^%@%$^$ phone company that doesn't even list its own phone number.

+7:50 – Wife reminds you that phone company changed its name seven years ago. Find phone number under old name.

+7:55 – Call The Old Company With A New Name "telecommunications service." Wait in queue. Hear message saying: "Please have your account number on hand for better service."

+8:45 – Wife, looking at cell phone, announces that the US Women scored their first goal.

+8:55-12:59 – Wait in phone queue and listen to messages urging you to buy more services. Wonder if they offer a premium service to avoid waiting in phone queues.

+13:00 – Operator answers, asks how she can help? Tell her you need your 16-digit number.

+13:05 – Hear operator say "Our account numbers are not 16-digits."

+13:10 – Argue. Tell her you know better. Tell her you simply MUST have your satellite number.

47

+13:15 – Hear her say "OK, but I don't think I can get that for you."

+13:20 – Tell her that the Old Peacock People want that number, and she'd better give it up or someone is going to get hurt.

+13:30 – Hear her say "Buddy, I've worked here for 30 years, and no one has ever asked me for that."

+13:40 – Acknowledge uniqueness of the situation but remind her that YOU MUST GET THAT NUMBER OR YOU CAN'T WATCH THE OLYMPICS."

+13:50 – Endure a long silence, be told that she CAN connect you to the Saucer People, but she "can't promise you that they'll give you the number."

+14:05 – You ask her to connect you anyway.

+14:15 – Hear phone ring, listen in amazement as a Live & Friendly Human Being answers. Hear him say "How may I help you?" Pray this is not a wrong number.

+14:30 – Babble that you "need the magic number that will let you watch our hometown hero play soccer on the Internet."

+14:40 – The Live & Friendly Human Being laughs, and assures you he can help. You experience hope and euphoria.

+14:45 -15:00 – You are entrusted with the magic 16-digit number.

+15:15-18:30 – The Live and Helpful Human being TALKS YOU THROUGH screen after screen of questions. You eventually click on the end-user, "EULA" agreement, which gives the Saucer People permission to claim your oldest child during half-time.

+19:00 – YOU'VE NOW GOT A SAUCER ONLINE ACCOUNT AND ARE READY TO WATCH LIVE SOCCER.

+19:05-20:25 – You find that, after being on the Saucer Site, you don't know how to get back to OLD PEACOCK WEBSITE.

+20:30 – You tell your wife that you don't like her #*&<%P^6! browser and all things created by Bill Gates. Wife avoids eye contact, sits quietly in the corner of the room, looking at her cell phone.

+20:35-21:00 – You hunt, peck, and claw your way back to the OLD DEAD BIRD logo.

+21:10 – You're met with a blank, black screen and ominous message: "May

Need a Plug-In Update." You put aside dark thoughts of Bill & Co. and copy the Live Olympic Coverage URL and CLOSE MICROSOFT EXPLORER.

+21:20 – With relief, you launch "Your-Favorite-Browser-That-Wasn't-Made-By-Bill-Gates."

+21:25 – Finally, you paste URL into the YFBTWMBBG browser. And PRESTO! ... Another black screen.

+22:40 – You see warning that the Old Peacock website needs the latest Twinkle-video plug-in.

+24:00 – You click on "Update Plug-In Instructions."

+24:05 – Then click on Uninstall the "Twinkle Plug-in."

+24:45 – Click on link to download the "NEW BUT ESSENTIALLY THE SAME TWINKLE PLUGIN."

+25:30 – Download complete, begin installation.

+25:45 – Watch installation progress, realize you've accidentally downloaded additional pay-software that will over-write your free anti-virus software, ABORT! ABORT DOWNLOAD!

+26:00 – Get re-Twinkled, again, san virus checker.

+26:30 – Install new plug-in.

+27:00 – Paste Old Peacock URL into YFBTWMBBG/Twinkle enabled.

+27:15 – Almost there! See Screen directing you to Saucer Online.

+27:30 – Get into the Saucer.

+27:45 – Get "Sorry" screen that your Saucer subscription does not include... premium sports.

+28:00 – %$&$&$&$&$&###@$!

+28:10 – Notice offer on bottom of screen for a free, 4-hour trial subscription.

+29:00 – Complete subscription in wife's name using her soon-to-get-a-lot-of-spam email address.

+29:30 – Be forced to watch 2-minute Peacock commercial.

+32:00 – Begin watching the last few minutes of first half of the game. Hand computer to wife. Start to return to office to finish big-complicated-project. Accidently delete wrong file, losing two-hours of work.

+32:25 – Hear wife ask if her computer can be hooked to the Big-Screen TV.

+32:30 – Dig for cables in junk drawer to hook up wife's computer to TV.

+34:00 – Hook up computer to big screen TV. Unplug laptop from power supply because it won't reach. Notice that wife's computer battery is almost dead.

+34:15 – See browser crash.

+34:25 – Restart "$@&^%" browser.

+34:30 – Rewatch the *same* 2-minute Peacock commercial.

+34:45 – See warning message. Decide to find extension cord for computer.

+36:45 – Actually see soccer players on our TV.

+37:00 – Find extension cord. It won't fit three-pronged computer plug.

+37:30 – Back to the junk drawer to find side-cutting pliers.

+38:00 – Mutilate extension cord so 3-plug computer plug can be jammed in.

+38:15 – Plug in computer, sit in office where you can see TV. Wonder if you have a backup to replace deleted file.

+38:20 – Wife shouts thank-you from the front room.

+39-41 – Hear excited sounds from front room, chants, cheering and the roar of the crowd on big screen.

+41:15 – Silence, browser crashes.

+42:00 – Error report sent. Restart browser.

+42-44 – Watch Peacock commercial for the third time.

+44-45 – Watch last minute of first half.

Halftime – Brower crash – reload – watch Peacock Commercial again. Realize you've spent more time watching this commercial than women's soccer.

Second half starts

+47 – Big screen freezes, bandwidth? Audio continues. Have to decide whether to just listen, or restart.

+49 – See error message pop up: "A script on this page is taking a long time. Do you want to wait?" Sound has stopped. Still no picture. You wait.

+50 – Restart, see Peacock commercial for 5th time. You now see why they let you watch this for free.

+51-91:59 – FINALLY. Wow. GO USA! Oh My God. NO. NO. NOOO. Whew. Nuts. GREAT SAVE. GO! GO! GO! Whew, that was close. "HEY REF??"

Finally – Watch your hometown gal win gold.

+92 – Sit down in chair, exhausted.

+93 Minutes – Hear wife say – "Wow. That was amazing." Admit that all the hassles were worth it to see our women in action. Console yourself that you can still see the parts you missed on the DVR—maybe....

+94 – Wife gets first spam solicitation from the "FREE OLYPMIC VIEWING."

SLEEPING WITH DARTH VADER

"Do you snore?" my doctor asked.

"Only when I sleep."

"Hmmm.... For how many years?"

This falls in the how-would-I-know category. *Really?* I'm asleep. He hands me a "sleep inventory" form to see if I have a "sleep disorder." I tick off my answers.

"Do you fall asleep while watching TV?"

Duh, who doesn't? That's why TVs have an auto-off timer.

"Do you fall asleep after eating a heavy meal?"

Sure, that's why they invented the Barcalounger.

I work my way down the list. After some more droll questions, the survey gets down to matters of life-and-death. Specifically "Do you fall asleep behind the wheel of your car?" NO, and "Have you fallen asleep while your wife was talking to you?" Left blank.

The doctor returned and took the clipboard.

"I never have trouble falling asleep," I said.

He studied the form "Hmm...."

"And nothing wakes me up at night."

"But you have afternoon fatigue," he said, tapping question number seven.

"Yeah, that's why I got a referral."

"Your blood work is OK."

"That's good," I said, feeling encouraged. Then, he rolled his chair over to me, and massaged my neck. "Hmmm…." He looked at more of my responses. "You may be a candidate for a sleep study." He looked up. "Here," he said handing me yet another paper to fill out. "You can complete this when you talk with your sleep partner."

Partner? I'd never thought of my wife as partner in that sense, mainly because we sleep so differently. I thought SHE was the one with a problem. She struggles to sleep. I swear, someone eating marshmallows in the kitchen it would keep her awake. Most nights she watches late-night TV to drift off. This, in turn, gives her Technicolor nightmares. I know this because she talks, no shouts, in her sleep. But it's not all bad, if Letterman's a rerun, I can switch off the set and just listen to her. Recently she started shouting "GRACIE ALLEN. GRACIE ALLEN," as though it was the winning answer in a game show.

But I did what the doctor ordered, and asked her about my snoring.

"I snore?"

She stared at me like I'd grown a third eye. "Hello? I turn you on your side each night."

I did seem to remember a loving elbow every now and then.

"When did I start?"

"Ask your dad," she said shaking her head sadly. "You've snored since day one." She shot me that long-suffering of a woman carrying more than her share of marital baggage. "I don't complain because I know you can't help it."

Now I felt bad. So we completed the form, and I did a sleep study. This is where total strangers videotape you while you're in bed, and, no, this is not done in a cheap hotel. On top of this, I had more wires attached to me than an FBI informant. At the end of it all, I got the bad news.

"You had 38 episodes an hour," the doctor said. As a performing arts teacher, this sounded good, until he explained that I had basically stopped breathing every minute or two.

"Really?"

"Yes," he said, "and your oxygen level…" he showed me a long paper printout, "dropped below 80%." He said that when 'blood-ox' goes below 80%, you're unconscious.

"That's why I sleep so well."

"But you're NOT sleeping properly." He pointed to some other squiggles, and explained disrupted REM. Even worse, serious, long-term problems result from oxygen deprivation. Then I made the mistake of asking why this was happening, and he told me. It's because I have "an unusually large tongue. But the good news," he added cheerfully, "is you don't need surgery." I flinched.

Instead, I got a CPAP machine. This contraption pumps air into my throat to keep it open. I was explaining this to my kids, what it looked like and how it worked, by telling them it was like a cool, jet-fighter pilot's mask. But my kids had trouble forming a mental picture.

"Tell them you look and sound like Darth Vader," my wife said, smiling. "But at least you quit snoring ."

LAWN CARE FOR THE HORTICULTURALLY IMPAIRED

I've been asked to share a few tips on yard care to be included in the upcoming eBook, "101 Things Totally Inept People Do To Screw Up Their Lawns." I was glad to contribute since I'm an expert in this area, and because it kept me from actually having to go outside and mow.

Avoiding yard work can be difficult and takes years of training, practice and planning. In fact, it can take up to three years before your newborn is able to operate a power mower. Each of my four children can attest to this. Sadly, though, at one time or another, they've all accused me of having kids just to press them into Bermuda-grass-bondage. This is totally untrue. The reason we had them, of course, was so I could coach soccer and have a socially acceptable reason not to mow my lawn on Saturday afternoons. But let's get down to the finer points of yard care.

First, in most climates, a well-designed automatic watering system is a must. I can tell you this with absolute certainty because I installed one in our side-yard. I made dozens of trips to Mr. Hammer Hardware, the huge warehouse that sells PVC pipe, valves, sprinkler heads, Hubba-Bubba Bubble Gum and free kittens. I spent hundreds of dollars on thousands of pieces of high-tech plastic that I took home and dumped in the middle of my driveway. After all this exhausting shopping, I went inside to fix myself lunch and give the new kitten to my son, hoping all the while that the yard gnomes and sprinkler fairies would come and assemble it for me. When that didn't happen, I spent the next two days exploring a few dozen of the three gazillion possible plumbing configurations. But it's really pretty easy, if you've spent years playing with Tinker Toys.

I glued it all together and then marveled at my handiwork; after all, I'd read three different instruction manuals, consulted with Karl from Mr. Hammer, and crafted a masterpiece. Shortly afterward, though, I realized that it needed to be buried in the ground to work properly.

Only kidding, I never read the instructions. But when I was done, I had a fully automated system that ... had no water pressure. Indignant, I went back to Mr. Hammer to complain.

"My sprinklers don't work."

"Ahhh," Karl rubbed his chin. "Have you checked the anti-backflow valves to make sure they're not backwards?"

"Ahhh," I rubbed my chin. "Backwards anti-backflow."

"Have you properly programmed your zone timer?" Karl asked. "Allowing for the difference between Greenwich Mean Time, Daylight Savings, and the standard deduction for a two-income household?"

"Ahhh," I nodded. "Zone GMT, DST and 1040a?"

Karl smiled. "You didn't read the directions."

I was indignant. "Do you mean the directions that came with the valves? The ones that came with the multi-function controller or the ones that came with the sprinklers?"

"You read all that?" He was awed.

"No, but I did read the comic in my Hubba-Bubba."

So it turns out that there is a formula for calculating water pressure over distance, and that hooking a new system to an old one that is about the size of a drinking straw is Not A Good Idea.

"It' a common problem," Karl said.

So, I got to dig it all up, buy many more pieces of plastic, and start over. This made me something of an expert in the art of underground yard art.

The other trick to simplified-lawn-maintenance is surprisingly easy. Encourage your wife to get a dog.

Now, you may be saying: "But dogs and lawns don't mix." How wrong you are! First, a dog is a great reason not to mow the lawn. I learned this when I first stood behind my Dad's REO. This motorized push mower had one forward speed just under that of a dragster, and it had the charming habit of tossing trimmings right in your face. This was fun when it was body parts from my sister's

Barbie. Not so much fun when it was pulverized poop from the family pooch. The lesson here is that you can always walk out to the yard, look around, and then and say, "Well, I WAS going to mow the lawn, but someone needs to clean all this up."

This can keep you away from mowing for years.

Second, if you get the right dog, it will just remove your lawn for you, one piece at a time. We now have Lucy, a lovable Anatolian Shepherd/Great Pyrenees mix who is a digger. That is, she loves to create her own cool spots in the yard. She does this by excavating holes the size of a small bus. Once she has created a space, she decides it would be even more fun to make another little nest over in a shady spot on the other side of the yard. After a year of this, we now have a landscape that looks like it was made by the people who design displays for NASA's Moon Rocks.

But if you're not lucky enough to get a Lucy, the odds are still pretty good that you can get one that will do the job indirectly. I know this because we had Radar, a golden retriever with keen canine instincts, sharp teeth, and the digestive systems of a goat. Radar-the-dog-genius ate the key components of our sprinklers, and in no time at all, yard care became quite simple. The lawn took on the finer features of burnt toast. The bushes withered, and my wife's beloved cherry tree croaked.

What could be easier?

So, in closing, if you want to picture yourself on a beautiful, well-trimmed lawn, become a soccer coach. Or, you can do what my 79-year-old-father does. Go to Sears and get the latest in high-tech care—a cordless vacuum to clean your plastic grass.

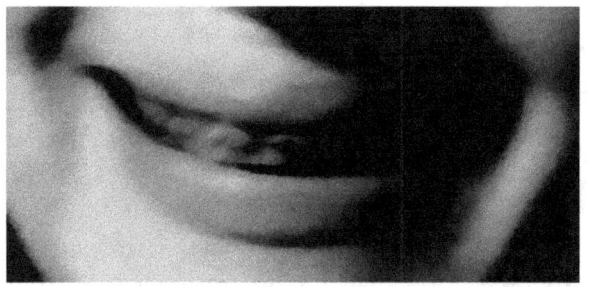

WHAT THE TOOTH FAIRY WON'T TELL YOU

When I was a child, the dentist's office was a strange place that poked you with needles, said "everything will be OK," and then filled your head full of shrapnel that we now know causes Global Warming. But you weren't worried about losing teeth, since this was a major source of kid-income.

Ah, but how times have changed. Now, the dentist is a place to go to help you learn about the latest advances in molar technology. Trust me, there's always huge advances between visits, especially if your last checkup was back when Jimmy Carter was president. You have a vast array of choices to remove decaying currency from your wallet before you do something foolish and harmful to your dorsal-lingual retainers, like buying food.

The sad fact is that secrets of proper dental care are not entrusted to children. This epiphany came just after I turned 30, and a deeply-disappointed technician said that I could expect all my teeth to fall out in the next five minutes or so. I was a bit shocked. After all, my parents had told me throughout my childhood that if I brushed twice a day, I was good to go. Not that I did this, mind you, but I thought as long as I believed it, and agreed with the dentist each visit, then I'd get a pass much in the way you clear customs by lying through your teeth.

But once you become an adult you're told that you'd better start flossing. Actually, you're told that you should have been flossing for the past 40 years and you can expect to suffer unspeakable pain for your lack of proper care. It's true. Once you see the bill it will make your teeth ache.

I had many reasons for avoiding the dentist. First, plenty of TV commercials prove, scientifically, that sugar-free gum fights decay. That's good enough for me. Then there was the trauma of looking like Alvin-the-Chipmunk after my wisdom teeth were yanked. Not to mention that, as an adult, I had to pay the tab. But, finally, the day came when I grew up, got serious, extracted insurance coverage from my employer, and started a long-term relationship with the people in white lab coats.

I'm happy to report I have a whole dental-services-team trying to resuscitate my bicuspids. In fact, my dentist has more people working for her than now work for General Motors. There's my dentist, of course, and we'll talk more about this amazing woman in a moment, but we must also recognize the unsung heroes who labor down in plaque-filled trenches each day, fighting a never-ending battle against gingivitis.

I'm referring, or course, to the hygienists. One of the most tactful people in the world is the woman who makes the appointment to clean my teeth. Then, of course, there's the other hygienist who actually does the scraping because hygienist #1 is always unavailable. Hygienist #2 assures me that it has nothing to do with me accidentally trying to bite hygienist #1 after she accidentally tried to jab me during a dental procedure. Aside from this, I really feel sorry for my hygienist. Each time we meet, she has her hopes dashed after the exam. "We're losing ground," she shakes her head. I feel guilty, and I promise to try harder. Encouraged, she tries to coach me on how to floss better, and how to properly use the new electric toothbrush, water pick and special anti-plaque mouthwash. This process is repeated at each cleaning. But I must admit, I've found this regimen surprisingly easy. Really. I do it first thing in the morning, and when I'm through, it's time to go back to bed.

Next, of course, is technology-man. He's the guy who maintains their state-of-the-art computer-controlled drills, water pick and Shop Vac. He has something to do with the electronic wall art that looks suspiciously like X-Rays. I have never met him, but I hear him discussed in hushed reverence. So hushed, I couldn't tell you his name.

Another key member of the team is the accountant, Mike, whose job it is to look concerned and tell me the "procedure" I most need is probably not going to be covered by the insurance. Procedures are less frightening as surgery, but more expensive. It works like this. Mike calls insurance to double-check just as I pull into the parking lot, and they always call him back during the procedure when I'm too happy to care. But Mike's resourceful, kind and encouraging. He tells me not to worry, that it may be "covered under another billing code," such as that for a sex-change operation. According to their records, I'm the first person to have 12 such procedures. This could explain why I like to read *Field & Stream* while watching chick flicks.

Then there's the receptionist, who has both the most unpleasant AND the most difficult jobs of all. She has to see me twice. First, when I enter, she's the one who hands me a stack of "updated forms." It seems that this is cheaper than having a bunch of tattered magazines. It's certainly more entertaining. I read the forms. I complain. I snarl. I fume. But it makes absolutely no difference. She nods sympathetically, and then shrugs. Apparently, my dentist's team includes a dozen attorneys who specialize in disclosures. It occurs to me that this should make me nervous just about the time the painkillers kick in.

I also see the receptionist on my way out. I'm numb now, and can't talk. This, of course, is a definite improvement. But now she's tasked with the most difficult job in the entire operation, one that takes more skill and finesse than anything else in the medical profession. Now she has to make sure I show up on time for my next appointment. This process begins when she hands me a card with a dated, detachable molar-sticker. But that's just the start. From there, her behavior entails what, in other circumstances, would be considered stalking. I get reminders via snail mail, texts, email, and even a chipper phone call. I'm convinced they saved part of my anesthesia for her.

But quality care really comes down to the trust and respect, which is to say fear, I have of my dentist.   Most of what an uninformed public thinks about dentists is unfair and unkind. They're not in the back room, looking at your X-Rays, while studying a Mercedes-Benz flyer. This would be both unprofessional, and oh so1990s. What they're doing now is looking at your financial statement and drooling over a Bass-Boat catalog. (Hey attorneys, only kidding.)

But despite all the changes I've seen, I still have to wonder what they do with all the teeth they pull. They won't give them to you. I know, because I've asked. They're considered "biohazards." The teeth, not the dentists. Still, I'd like to have mine back as they drop out so I can tuck them under my pillow.

With all I've invested, I expect to wake up and find a BMW.

THE GARBAGE MAN COMETH

PROLOGUE: The following is a mostly-true story pulled from the files of the Sanitation Squad. The events described here actually happened, but the names have been removed to protect the not-so-innocent.

The Place: *Palo Cedro, Shasta County. Not a bad place to live if you like skunks and coyotes.*

The Time: *Tuesday morning before dawn. Sounds from the street disturb the neighborhood ...*

VAROOOOMMMM…
SCREEECH…. BEEP…. BEEP….
BEEP…… WHAM…. WHIRR….

Oh-Dark-Thirty I awake, and realize… IT'S GARBAGE DAY. I jump out of bed, race to the window, and peer down the driveway into pitch-blackness. "DID ANYONE PUT THE CANS OUT?"

Silence… except for an idling diesel engine…. Suddenly, I see that I have a *who-should'a-done-it* mystery on my hands.

∗∗

Story begins the previous Monday. Suppertime. Lightfoot kitchen. My name's Robb. My Partner's Karin. We're parents, and we carry a mortgage.

We were working night-shift on the counter near the stove. Making dinner. It's quiet, one of those evenings when the town takes a deep breath and holds it, just waiting to exhale trouble. Then it happens.

"What's wrong, Robb?"

"Somethin'."

"What?"

"Dunno. Just a sense I got."

I look about, and then I see it. The trash can. It's full. More than full. Overflowing. It reeks.

"Hmmm…. Suspicious in-activity." I say, and signal my partner to cover for me. I cruise into the front room to work the case.

Dangerous place, the TV district. I see the usual suspects. Four of them, splayed out on the couch and floor. Watching. Up to no good. Strung out on reruns. They ignore me. Probably should call for backup. Then I recognize the leader. Known in these parts as the trash man.

"Hey (name redacted)…. You still doin' the garbage?"

An almost-lifelike form stirs. "Uhhhh."

"Don't make me get tough here. Is that a 'yes,' or a 'no'?"

The subject's eyes shift, and then roll.

"Later, Dad." The volume on the TV set increases.

Years of cop-shows and parenting, which share much in common, guide my interrogation.

"Meaning that you'll tell me *later*? You'll decide *later*? Or you'll do it *later*?

Subject scowls, and then shrugs. I take this as a negative response. The others slink into the shadows.

"So that's the way you want it?" I pull up a chair. "OK. I've got as long as it takes."

Silence.

"Not the first time we've been here, right?" I say. "Easier if you cooperate."

"BUT I TOLD MOM ALREADY."

Hmmmm. Subject sought counsel? Incriminating.

"Right," I bark. "Mom's in the next room. Just wait here, and let's see if she gives you up."

Trash man takes the 5th, and I step back. Out of the corner of my eye I glimpse a furtive movement towards the can. STOMP. STOMP. STOMP. I smell a potential break in the case, I stop and turn on tough-cop. "Hey." I point at the others, "So give me a name. Wanna hang this on one of them?"

Ouch. An accomplice pulls a remote, and I'm shot with glaring eyes. Just a glancing ego wound. I return fire by flipping on the lights. Screams. Moans. Trash Man gives himself up. Trudges off.

"And while you're out, take the cans to the street," I snarl.

"It's dark."

"Yes," I say, "that happens each night."

"But it's scary, Daddy."

Ah.... the suspect is beginning to crack. "Well, good news kiddo. This week, no one's been roughed-up by rubbish."

"OK. BUT I'M BRINGING GRACIE!"

"Sure," I say, "Corrupt an innocent dog."

Subject grudgingly hauls garbage outside, bringing the family collie, Gracie.

This dog's not the sharpest knife in the drawer, but Gracie'll follow trash-man anywhere. I return to my station to check in with my partner.

"Learn anything?" Karin asks.

77

"Trash Man's on the move." I say.

"Yeah?" Karin asks.

"Yeah. May be a gang activity."

"Really?"

"Really." I say.

"Who?" she asks.

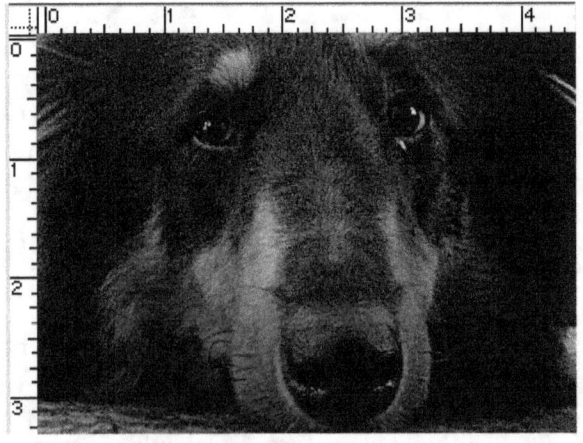

"Gracie," I say, "you know, the one with the small, beady eyes. Doggone shame."

Trash Man's gone a long time. Returns just at supper. No Gracie.

The lineup troops onstage for dinner. We see them face on, and then in profile. Chewing. Exercising their jaws and their right to remain silent. Trash man smiles wickedly but avoids eye contact.

Still no Gracie.

Despite repeated questions from my partner and me, we're unable to ascertain if cans were moved to the street or Gracie's whereabouts.

Suspicious.

TO BE CONTINUED....

✳✳

EPILOGUE: *Tuesday Morning, O-Dark-Thirty plus two.*

I race to the street . Cans are out. Sweet Smell of Success. Score one for the Sanitation Squad, Special Parent Unit.

I head back to the house, past our garage.

Light's on. Hmmmm.... Better check it out.

Looking in. Nothin's amiss. But then...

A mournful whimper...

An unmistakable odor...

"WHO PUT A SKUNKED DOG IN MY LAUNDRY ROOM!?"

Time to rouse the usual suspects.

TOYING WITH TROUBLE

Uncle Joe bought me my bazooka. He lived 3,000 miles away, in Detroit. I don't think he could hear the explosions, but I'm not sure. He quit calling us after Christmas.

That Sonic Blaster was one of two presents from my "Genius Uncle," as Mom called him. The other was the "Big Ear" eavesdropping dish. Mom confiscated it immediately. This seems an odd choice. You'd think that she'd have appreciated the peace and quiet afforded by "the Ear" over the Blaster's glass-rattling explosions.

My parents were remarkably patient people. But it took them a while to discover our fundamental philosophical difference. They thought that toys were supposed to be fun and buy them a few moments of peace. I thought that my toys were tools of discovery, or war, depending on where you stood. Standing far away was usually a good idea.

Some of their gifts they soon regretted – toy saws that really cut wood, pocket knives and magnifying glasses. I blamed them. They were the adults, and it really was their fault when I torched leaves, incinerated bugs, or modified our furniture to better fit a family of Munchkins.

Take the "Bangsite Cannon." This 18-inch piece of artillery fell into my possession when I was 10. It used the same gas that fuels a cutting torch.

The cannon's operating instructions said to "put two teaspoons of water in the barrel. Dip plunger into 'Bang-site compound' available at toy stores everywhere! Insert assembly into breech, rotate, count to 10. Depress plunger smartly."

"Smartly" in this case means rapidly; it does not reflect the wisdom of giving an explosive device to a hyperactive boy.

I loved the cannon. It made a bigger bang than grandpa's backfiring Studebaker. But soon the noise was just boooring. I looked at that barrel, and it wasn't enough just to *imagine* a shell flying from it into an enemy camp. It needed more oomph, so I applied "plaything-synergy." This is done by combining toys in unintended, forbidden or unimagined ways.

I transformed my Tinkertoys, a sedate set of sticks, into missiles. Here's how it's done. Grab a stubbie, a Tootsie-Roll-shaped cylinder, tack on a red tip for aerodynamics, and insert into the cannon's barrel... Voila! You've got an artillery shell.

The first volley was so-so. It flew over the house and bounced off the dog.

Further work was in order. In a short time, I discovered that TWO stubbies, connected with a yellow shaft, were the ticket. This setup had stability and heft. Better yet, it looked cool, and felt like a real weapon, one to strike fear in the hearts of our neighbors and other enemies.

Sadly the newer, bigger, better bombshell would barely go across the front yard. It did put a cool looking dent in Dad's old Chevy, but it needed more "go-power."

Dad always said: "When all else fails, read the directions." And he was so right! Instructions *are* the place to look for innovative methods only dimly anticipated by the manufacturer. Just remember that they're *suggestions*, not hard-and-fast rules.

So, I saw, in big red type, a cautionary note to "**NEVER USE MORE THAN ONE SCOOP OF THE BANGSITE SOLUTION**." There were words I didn't understand like "excessive gas"… "injury to the operator." But what caught my eye was the "risk of explosion."

Of course, we needed an *explosion*— that's what powered the moon shots! So I doubled the charge. It helped. Tripling worked even better. I was back in business.

Scientific advances, though, often have setbacks and misfortune. Bad luck, in this case, arrived in the form of my kid sister. She came. She saw. She ratted me out. Little Sis dragged Mom into the front yard in time to witness the full glory of triple-charged Bangsite power applied to multi-stage-Tinkertoy technology.

It was a beautiful sight, that missile streaking nearly a city block. But Mom freaked, and that was the end of my cannon. Grownups have pitifully little appreciation for novel ideas. So somewhere out there in the

Twilight Zone sits a shelf full of long lost toys. My beloved cannon rests next to all the other cool stuff that was taken to keep me from killing myself.

Did Mom do the right thing? Who knows. Letting me be could have led to a benign but helpful career in applied physics, demolition, or the infantry. But she meddled, and I became an English major. So instead I'm both dangerous *and* useless.

CELL MATES

This summer was particularly exciting for us. My brother and one of my daughters earned BA degrees. My wife and I celebrated 30 years of marriage. And in a once-in-a-lifetime alignment of the planets, not one but two of our family's cell phones are eligible for an upgrade.

It's a time of reflection and negotiation. Among the five of us, who'll get the upgrades? Will it be daughter #3, since her old flip-phone is disintegrating from constant use? Or should it be daughter #2, whose phone is lovingly called "Retro"? This phone came out of mothballs to replace one that her friend tossed in the river because it was "way uncool." This "helpful" friend remains alive today only because I never managed to get his name.

My family, my cell mates. We share the same plan, but we have different phone-philosophies. My method – leave it off and return the call later. I hear this is "old school." Daughter #3's approach is to answer on the second ring, at all times, anytime, every time. Daughter #2 won't return a call for days, but will text you in a few minutes if you text her. Our son's voicemail has been full for years now. He answers only if he's texted first, and my wife couldn't do her job as a nursing teacher without her cell. She's very good about returning calls, this is partly because her i-Have-A-Better-Phone-Than-You possesses a psychic friends feature that dials out randomly for no apparent reason.

Still, we're grandfathered in at "low rates," a reward for 20 years of paying for service we'd lived without our entire lives—BCP, Before Cell Phones. Our first "portable" had the size and heft of a brick, only uglier. The technology was "analog," which means that it emitted enough power to soft-boil your brain if you talked on it for more than five minutes.

This was a very, very special phone that was off almost all the time, to save the battery. It stayed on only during those rare evenings when my wife and I hired a babysitter and went out to dinner. This allowed our sitter to ensure that every unpleasant thing we were paying her to deal with was relayed to us almost instantly. What a joy it was to be asked, during dinner, if there was any trick to getting cat vomit off our new couch. As the children grew, they soon were old enough to be home alone. We stopped getting babysitter calls. Instead we'd get the pay-per-view experience, where one kid would call from a safe distance and narrate the blow-by-blow fight unfolding in the next room. The audio on our phone wasn't the full digital quality we know today, so the screams could only be heard one or two tables away. Next, when the kids were old enough to drive, we gave each a cell phone for their safety and Mom's peace-of-mind. Of course, what that meant is Dad got service calls from people who thought that the "E" on the gas gauge was only a suggestion, or who heard a funny noise that went away after I'd abandoned my Barcalounger, drove 20 miles, and raised the hood.

Cell phones, for my money, mean calls from people with problems who *want* my money. Back when I was a kid, people needing money had the decency to call you "collect," and you could always refuse the charges. Such is progress. Now our phone bill costs enough that no one can afford to go out. It rivals the payments on my first house, but no matter what, everyone seems to covet a new phone. My son may have just gotten the Watoosee 500, but he now needs the new 500S. It talks to you, can play games, surf the web, and ignore a call all at once. "And, Dad, you get this $700 phone for 'only' $300."

Or, my daughter tells me, I can get a "free" phone for "only $100."

"Free?"

"Yeah, but I need a car charger, skins, multimedia kit, scratch guards, and carry case," she says.

Oh, joy. Upgrade? Please just lock me in a cell, preferably one with lots of padding and zero bars.

THE WORLD'S WORST MOVIE

Darkness. Disgust. Dyspepsia. And we're only 10 minutes into *Pokémon*.

I'm trapped in Movies 8, feet stuck to the floor, watching. My three kids giggle. I groan. Next door, my wife, Karin, and our oldest daughter are watching Bruce Willis actually die in a movie. But I drew the short straw. So, here I sit, with a bucket of butter and a gawd-awful film.

My head hurts.

Then it hits me. This movie is so bad that it's rotting my forebrain. It must be. I stare at the screen and bizarre, brightly-colored anime creatures flit about. Looking away, I spy another zombified adult. I've seen that face in *Invasion of the Body Snatchers*.

Much, much later, I rejoin my wife in the lobby. "So, Hon," I growl. "WHAT'S THE WORST MOVIE YOU'VE EVER SEEN?" I give her a subtle glare.

"Worse than *The Three Stooges*?" she asks.

"Next to *Pokémon*, the Stooges are Masterpiece Theater." I feel a spasm of pain. "At the end, the characters' memories were erased." I rub my temples. "Lucky Pikachu."

Karin gives me a *you-took-one-for-the-team* hug, smiles, and tries to change the subject. "Did the kids like it?"

"The kids like Cap'n Crunch and Barney." My eye quit twitching. "That *THING* wasn't a movie. It was a feature-length video game ad."

"That bad?"

"It was THE WORST MOVIE I'VE EVER SEEN."

Karin was sympathetic, and eventually my brain began to work again. I was able to walk and ingest solids after just a few days.

Yet I was wrong about Pokémon, Pikachu, and Squirt-thing. They're not as bad as it gets. I revised my opinion when the kids got older and I was duped into seeing *The Matrix*. This film put science education back two decades. If you missed it because you were doing something more worthwhile and fun, like eating lint, let me explain. This is set in a world where all the energy we need is sucked out of your recumbent body and fed into ...THE MATRIX. Got that? But you don't care because your mind is wired into virtual reality provided by... THE MATRIX. If you don't like this arrangement, you can opt out and take a red pill. Then they escort you to the box office and give you your money back.

I wish.

No. If you're like me, you can't move because you're with family and spilled soda has crazy-glued your shoes to the floor. So you sit and hope to see a plot kick in or some credible acting burst forth. You'd even settle for significant theme sneaking onstage. The credits roll before any of this happens.

Yet lots of people love this movie. My son is one of them.

"Why?" I asked.

"Really, Dad? Just because it's got really cool high-speed filming with real industrial-grade cameras. You know? For really-slow-motion."

And so it does. Really.

I know this because he spent the entire summer at home with a DVD watching the bullets-being-dodged *FRAME-BY-FRAME*. The director could have saved a ton of money and not missed a beat of the plot, since there wasn't any, if he'd just run the bullet bit as a loop for, say, three months.

Now I'm old fashioned. I expect characters to be more interesting than special effects. But I admit that technology has helped make movie going easier. Once we had to drive to the theater, hand over a fistful of cash, and risk seeing a terrible movie. Now we have DVDs, Netflix, satellite, a big-bundled-monthly-bill, and we're *guaranteed thousands of terrible films*. Ah, progress. Remember video stores? They used to have remainder bins full of these movies that went "straight to video." But the odd thing is that someone, somewhere, with popcorn-scorched gustation, liked the film enough to spend a mondo-million bucks to make it.

Now that the kids are out and about, my wife and I are often left to make our own movie picks. This would seem to improve the odds getting something we both enjoy. Not necessarily. I've been told that I am not to be trusted with the remote control or the Netflix "queue." Apparently, I can be the guy with the remainder-bin taste buds.

For example, I like *Ma and Pa Kettle, You Can't Take It With You, It's a Mad, Mad, Mad World,* and *What's Up Doc?* I relish an evening with low-budget 1950s horror films. Finally, I can watch them without having to hide in the back of the theater, peering over a seat. Now I just hit pause and turn on all the lights. But when I look around, I find myself alone.

Karin can take just so much before she bails.

I do try to watch movies with my wife, but her taste runs more to dog flicks. We watched *Marley and Me,* a story about the worst dog in the world. A fun movie, I'll admit, but mostly because it made our dogs look not all THAT bad.

Sadly, not all mutt movies are good.

The next bit of canine cinema we saw, thanks to the magic of Netflix, is now top contender for The Worst Movie Ever....

Hachi.

I can see why this flick put its tail between its legs and fled the theater. It has three problems. First, it's got Richard Gere in it. Second, it DOESN'T have Julia Roberts. And third, it features one of the most dim-witted pooches to ever slobber on stage. Proof? Gere spends an hour of screen time, or 7-Gere-Years, teaching this dog to fetch. This appears to be a major accomplishment for both man and dog.

Spoiler alert. In Hachi, Gere doesn't bed the fetching female lead. It's not that type of movie. It might be better if it was.

Once he teaches Hachi to retrieve a squeaky yellow ball, Gere gets on a train and never returns. Some may say that this improves the film. I wouldn't know. I fell asleep. But my wife assures me that the ending was pensive. She cried, and offered to watch it again with me. I declined. Instead, I rented *Where the Red Fern Grows* to clear the *Hachi-odor* out of our house.

Karin's quick to defend *Hachi-The Dog That Waited* against all attackers, especially me. She argues that *The Hot Tub Time Machine* is the worst. I'm in no position to disagree, since my son talked her into seeing this horrible (she says) film while I wasn't around. My son still enjoys sleeping in our hot-tub, so the movie couldn't be THAT bad.

95

Yes, there are plenty of great movies out there that both my wife and I like. The *Wizard of Oz* entertains and offers memorable characters. *North by Northwest* and *The Birds* continue to make us sit on the edge of our seats. We laugh and cry every time we see *Steel Magnolias*. And just recently, we were pleasantly surprised by Eddie Murphy in *A Thousand Words*.

Still, the remainder bins overflow with stinkers, and the aroma lingers.

But what *IS* The Worst Movie In The World? It's hard to agree. There's so many contenders that I think we need to break it down by category. Here's my pick of the worst pics.

Worst children's movie? How about *Mac and Me*?

Worst first-date movie? Definitely *History of the World Part* I.

Worst comedy? Anything with Adam Sandler.

Worst Western? *ALL OF THEM.* Right?

Worst Horror Film, in the special unintentionally-funny category? I'll have to do more research when Karin's not around and get back to you. It's a tough call.

We've come a long way since *Teenage Zombies*. Despite competition from abroad, Tinsel-Town still slaps together the best horrible horror films.

If only they could make the price of popcorn less frightening.

MINIMAL EFFORT VOTING

A PUBLIC SERVICE ANNOUNCEMENT

Hi, this is Max Inertia, your host of *Better Living Through Minimal Effort*. We invite you to stay tuned—it's easier. Today's guest is Ms. Bee Fuddled, Director of the League of Perplexed Voters. Bee, the election's just days away, and we don't want to hear more debates or wade through a voter's guide bigger than the LA phone book. What do you suggest?

Max, we all like to *seem* highly-educated. But who has 27-hours-a-day to watch TV? Fortunately, there are shortcuts.

Great. What are they?

For simplicity, I'd recommend the "Traditional Approach."

How does that work?

Seek out your family's traditions. Since no one's got time to read *all* the supermarket tabloids, pick your family's brains—there's usually not much to look through.

OK, Bee. The lines are open. Let's hear what our listeners say.

Plenty, I'll bet. Granddad always told me how to vote.

We have a caller from Red Bluff. Bob, you're on *Minimal Effort*. Got a tip?

Yeah, Max, my Dad had a fool-proven way of decidin'-on them ballot propositions by just lookin' at the name. If it was a vowel, a consonant or a number divisible by one, he'd vote HELL NO.

Thanks, Bob. Line two is Anita-Lynn from Anderson. What's your voting tradition?

My mother taught me to use the Teddy-Bear system, Max. You just think about which guy you'd like to see with his cute little head on your pillow. Then, you imagine the lights going down... Me, I like a furry, gentle-man...

Ah... Thanks, and back to you, Bee. I hear the League has proposals for electoral reform.

Yes, ideas to shorten elections, cut costs, and increase voter turnout.

Such as?

The League-sponsored "Presidential Cage Match." Candidates lose the suit and don the Spandex. Apply grease, and let them get slippery with the current WWF Heavyweight Champ.

Scoring?

Shortest post-match hospital-stay wins.

Any other ideas, Bee?

There's the Health Care Faceoff. Contenders are injected with H1N1, stripped of their insurance, and dropped into an inner-city ER. The ones who manage to get treated before the election win.

We have another caller from Redding. Hello, Jimmy. What's your family tradition?

Max, My Momma used "The Kiss of Death."

Is that legal?

Sure. Momma drove around town, past homes of people she hated. She'd scribble down the names on those yard-signs. Took that list into the booth... and voted *against* the lot of 'em.

Sounds complicated. Callers, we're looking for ideas that are truly zero-effort. Bee, while we're waiting... What else is the League proposing?

There's the Chinese-Checkers Shopping Spree. Actions speak louder than words, Max. So we give each candidate $500 and turn 'em loose for 15 minutes in Wal-Mart. Winner's cart has the most stuff made in the USA that supports education, the military or McDonald's.

OK, Bee.... Claudette from Mt. Shasta is on the line. What's your traditional tip?

Well, Grandma believed in the New Deal and Free-Love. She didn't discriminate on race, religion, or heart rate. She *always* wrote in "FDR."

A whole new take on vote the dead. Well, that about wraps it up for now. Bee, before we go, can *you* share one of your family traditions?

Sure, Max. I have two uncles. Dave's a businessman; Joe's a teacher. They call each other up, disagree on everything, and decide they'll cancel out each other's vote.

We must be related.

Well, one of them got the bright idea that they'd save time and money by not voting. They made a pact—each election they promise to stay home and "avoid all the hassle."

That's the *Minimal-Effort* motto.

Except... Max... They still vote.

A pity. Can I offer a quick suggestion?

Surely.

You didn't cover the environment. The League should try this. Take 50 middle-schoolers... Give each candidate a Swiss Army knife, 10 Happy Meals, and drop them all in the middle of San Diego's Safari Park. Winner would emerge with the most kids and the fewest monkey-bites.

Entertaining, Max.

And educational... Well, time to go... Thanks callers. Thanks Bee Fuddled. I'm Max

Inertia, and remember: If you think something is worth doing... Wait. The feeling *will pass.*

LOST AND FOUND

I love heartwarming headlines that reveal human nature. One such truth -- no matter how badly you've screwed up, there's always someone more inept.

Proof?

Minnesota's Moon Rocks Missing No More.

Ah, the "Gopher State," their motto? "'Star of the North' - Because We Can't Find

Our Moon Rocks." Their official mineral is reported to be "iron ore," but we can't be sure because someone mislaid the sample.

But no more shame. All is forgiven. The moon rocks turned up in a storage facility for military artifacts. I'm sure this makes perfect sense to people who spend half their time standing in shorts, knee-deep in snowdrifts.

Way to go, Minnesota! Wonderful news, and since these rocks were worth millions of dollars and disappeared for decades on somebody else's watch, I can now feel better about the time I lost $1 million for a week.

Yes, it really happened. No, I wasn't in Reno.

The story dates to the days I worked for a multi-national corporation and one of my employees made the money disappear with the push of a few buttons. I was an assistant branch manager at a place I'll call L.E.B., the Large-Evil-Bank. This L.E.B. location was only a small branch in the mountains. Sally, our button-banging NCR operator, shuffled up to me late one Friday afternoon with "a problem."

"I'm going to need some help closing out," Sally said.

"Don't you balance?"

"No," Sally said, "and it's a round number."

This meant, in banker's lingo, that it wasn't likely a "transposition error." Those numbers are always divisible by nine and easy to spot.

"How much?" I asked.

"I checked everything, a mil."

I thought that Sally had called the corporate help-line, known for its international staff, and talked to "Amil."

"What did Amil say?" I asked.

"Amil who?"

"Amil at corporate?"

"Who called her?" Sally asked.

"You did, right?"

"Why?"

"Over the difference. How much was it?"

"A *MIL*. I'M OUT A MILLION DOLLARS." Sally shouted.

Some sentences just hang in the air.

I stared at Sally—she stared back. I waited for her to smile, slap me on the back, and say she was "just funnin.'" After all, Sally was a practical joker, known for leaving baskets of black Easter Eggs on desks of people she disliked and putting Vaseline on doorknobs of the men's room. "Just to make 'em wash their damn hands."

Unfortunately, Sally was the same gal who, just two months before, had time-locked the vault while tens of millions of dollars in loan documents were sitting on our manager, CL's, desk.

He spent the weekend sleeping at the branch with his .45.

I looked at Sally, hoping she was kidding. She wasn't.

"What are we going to tell CL?" I asked.

"Oops?" Sally shrugged.

"How did it happen?"

Sally told her tale, a tragic-comic story of creative bookkeeping where one minor mistake was covered with another, slightly larger error. She'd repeated this process rapidly, working with nimble figures and diligence, until a cool million has vanished—on paper.

Sally and I presented ourselves to the manager, CL. He turned white.

"Are you calling the auditors?" I asked.

"Like hell," he said, eyes narrowing. "We're gonna find that money."

Six of us pored over every transaction that had rattled through the NCR machine Friday. Hundreds of them, totaling tens of millions of dollars. There were odd entries, as Sally had said, where she "plugged" numbers to force a balance. It was like trying to unmask a David Copperfield trick. The money just disappeared. Hours ticked by. Finally, we had to give up and release the bag of documents to our evening courier.

We "charged the difference to suspense," which is to say the branch loaned itself a million dollars. CL was furious, because we were now paying daily interest, to corporate, on a **MILLION DOLLARS**. The cost was taken from our tiny branch's profit.

"But the LEB hasn't lost anything," I said, hoping to calm CL. "Corporate gets paid."

"MY BONUS DEPENDS ON *OUR BRANCH'S* PROFITABILITY." He glared at me, and I shrank back to my desk.

So we didn't report the loss. We waited, biting our nails, for the money to turn up. Days went by, each time I saw the manager, he looked angrier, and I hoped he'd left his .45 at home. Finally, the "difference" kicked back from central accounting. Their computers found—and returned—the money.

But I had a l-o-n-g week of wondering how I'd explain to auditors, or people wearing uniforms, where the dough had gone. I hadn't a clue. This did factor into my decision that, maybe, banking wasn't the right job for me.

So, this week's headline gave me a warm, fuzzy feeling.

MINNESOTA'S MOON ROCKS MISSING NO MORE.

Minnesota fouled up big-time. Better yet, there are still 11 screw-up-states that lost moon rocks entrusted to them by Richard Nixon. I REALLY enjoyed reading this, one of the few times you'll see "trust" and "Richard Nixon" in the same sentence.

In closing, if you're ever having a bad day, like my Dad did when he left his truck in neutral and it drove itself into an oil sump, or my wife when she can't find either her blue-tooth earpiece OR her prescription reading glasses, just remember that you're doing better than the losers, Alabama, Louisiana, Nevada,

Massachusetts, South Carolina, Texas, Utah, Virginia, Washington, Wisconsin and the District of Columbia.

Take a bow. You survived, and you didn't get your name in the newspapers.

Way to go, Minnesota.

HALLOWEEN POINTERS

Pranksters in my neighborhood have just reached a new low. Someone TP'd a house—and did a pathetic job. First, they used heavy-duty paper towels, not the impossible-to-remove single-ply bargain-paper, and second, they forgot to soap the windows.

Really, people? Is this what America's youth has come to?

Realizing that valuable Halloween knowledge can be lost in just a single

111

generation, I'm passing along some valuable pointers.

Regarding Costumes - Remember if you can't find what you want in the store, you can always make your own. Karin is the master of this. One year we went as a lumberjack and a tree. She borrowed one of my flannel shirts, a knit cap, and a saw. I wore earth-toned clothes, a few branches and ran from her all night as she seemed pretty intent on using that saw to amuse our friends. Frightening your partner, one prankster point.

Another time, right after we were first married, she decided we should be Ma and Pa Kettle. She bought some plain long-johns and dyed them red. She carefully followed all the steps, including the part where she "set" the dye by tossing them in the apartment's communal dryer. What the instructions didn't say was that the process involves a bonus-prank. The next person to use the dryer gets an indelible hot-pink tint to their laundry, Cat-In-The-Hat style. Three points.

Treats, The Gifts That Keeps Giving -Karin, as a nurse, has issues with handing out candy. So, years ago, we bought boxes and boxes of raisins to give out instead. This is a great idea, since trick-or-treaters invariable look at them, wrinkle their noses, and toss them back at you. P.S. Be prepared to wash your windows the next morning. One point for each box not returned.

Pumpkins and Jack-O-Lanterns - You can thank the Irish for the wonderful tradition of carving pumpkins into frightening faces. The basic idea, if you're new to the planet, is Dad gives the kids an awkward, hard-to-handle gourd, a permanent marker, and a steak knife. Next, the kids scoop out the seeds and toast them in the oven. Set on broil until both smoke alarms sound off, then frost lightly with your fire extinguisher. Serves up two prankster points.

After the smoke clears, kids can then mutilate the poor pumpkin, using their parents' faces as models for the grimace. Finally, Dad fires up a Bic, lights a candle, and stuffs it down into the Jack-O-Lantern. Score one point if you burn the hair off your arm, three points if you have a father-daughter trip to the ER. Take away a point if you use the nurse-recommended safe-carving-tools and battery-powered lights.

Out and About - Halloween is when your kids are told to forget all that "not taking candy from strangers" stuff because, after all, Mom and Dad are standing right there. The problem is, if you're like us, you've probably caved and bought your tots the "hot" costume of the year. This means that there will be a dozen tiny Spidermen swarming on the porch like identical arachnids. So, when you return home, you may or may not have your own child. Think of it as an opportunity for a cultural exchange. Zero points for returning with your kids, two points each for the loaner-kids.

Candy – Worried that the idea of "free candy" sends the wrong message to little kids? Don't be. It's an opportunity to learn the power of bartering, when they have to trade four boxes of *Good-And-Plenty* for a *Zagnut* bar. It's also your parental duty to carefully examine each piece of candy, taking those that look suspiciously tasty. Score one point for each box of *Atomic Gobstoppers* you filch, negative two points for each drum of *Toxic Waste*.

Parties and Other Distractions - Back in the day, when our parents wanted a break from hauling us around, they'd drop us off at our church for a "Youth-Group Activity." This was like a regular Halloween party, but with the chance to give the pastor's car a potato-in-the tailpipe. The coed event allowed us to discover the difference between a Hershey's Kiss and a French kiss, and to see what other teens' undergarments looked like under a black light. Games included that wholesome, traditional activity using a barrel of water and a basket of apples—bobbing for mononucleosis. Two points for each kiss, negative five points for mono.

114

Too Old For T-O-T – My wife announced to the kids, when they reached high school, that they'd "aged out" of Trick-Or-Treating. This was a rude shock. There was pouting, yelling and screaming, and the kids didn't like it either. But they were shrewd and offered to take their younger siblings around, eliminating Mom and Dad's burden. Big sisters did this, "to be helpful." Then they smuggled out their own pillow cases, and managed to accumulate "payment-in-kind" carrying charges. Two points for ingenuity.

But then came the day when the music stopped. They were all too old to go. It wasn't pretty. They sulked on the sofa, and stared out the window, scowling. When the bell rang, I'd answer the door. Occasionally, it would be one of their classmates, and there would be a deep moan and a guttural cry.

"MOM! STEVE GETS TREATS!"

Steve. I'd heard of him. He had been in high school so long he had a reserved parking space. And there he stood, size 12 shoes, Levis, and a mangled shirt plastered with a bumper sticker that said: "Don't laugh mister, your daughter is in the back seat."

"Some costume," I said.

He grinned and held out his bag.

"Trick or treat, dude."

I dropped in a treat and slammed the door.

"IT'S NOT FAIR," said the chorus on the couch.

"OK, OK. Point taken," I said, firing a handful of goodies their direction. "Have some 20-year-old raisins."

Four points for Dad.

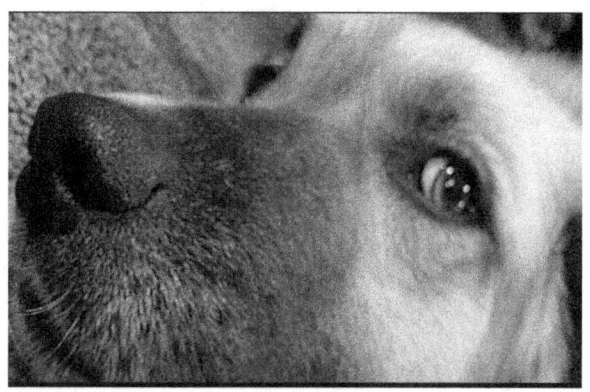

THE DOGGONE CHRISTMAS LIST

I'm working on "The Christmas List," and I can see Lucy, my wife's dog, watching me.

Now, Lucy's a pretty smart pooch. She realizes that when I put her on the leash, it's time to go to the vet. Rather than barreling down the driveway, she leads me to the car—she knows what's up.

So it's entirely possible that she sees "The List" and grasps its significance in just the same way that she understands the sound of food rattling into her bowl, or the sight of my wife pulling on running shoes before a walk.

I ponder, and Lucy comes over. Big brown eyes look deeply into mine, and she puts her Anatolian-Shepherd head on my knee. Maybe she's been reading my mind. It's been a tough year, and I'm wondering just how generous I can afford to be. Most of the kids are out of the house, so the fussing volume has subsided over the years. I can stop and reflect on the economics of gift-giving. Maybe I can dial it back a bit, but then there's this dog and its sustained stare.

I try to remember what the dogs got last Christmas. They have their own stockings, of course, and I seem to recall that they had a better year, stocking-wise, than I did. Not that I'm jealous or anything. I don't know that I really wanted jerky, a leather chew bone, or the studded collar. Well, not the chew bone anyway…

But the budget? Maybe I could kill a tradition, and hide the animals' stockings in the ornament box, buried under that hideous blue-and-green wreath. The wreath is another tradition, an heirloom given to us by a fashion-impaired relative. We never use it. I dare not give it away, and so it sits in the bottom of the box, year after year. This is, I think, the perfect hiding place. But, then, I'd have to explain to the wife why I neglected the critters. Nope. Not a pretty picture.

In my defense, I was in the pet store the other day, and I got stocking-stuffer shock. Even the cheap stuff seemed to be at least $5 a throw, or more. Then I did the math. You have to get each animal at least two--I think that's in the US Constitution somewhere. And it's not just the dogs, even the naughtiest cats get them. The expenses all add up.

Way, way up.

That's how things tend to happen around here. With four kids, pets for each of them, and a wife who never met a dog she didn't like, we're pushing double digits. The funny thing is that when the kids moved away, the animals remained. I'm not just talking about the ones buried in the backyard, I'm talking about the ones that are still walking around here, chewing up the upholstery and eating the houseplants.

A small voice in my head says, "Can't we start being practical?" Would the furry ones really miss being crossed off "The List?" I can definitely cut the cats. What would they care? Every day must seem like Christmas. Turn your back, and they're up on the counter feasting away. And doesn't it set a bad example to have them all jacked up on cat nip while we gather around the tree?

This is beginning to sound almost convincing, and then Lucy leans against me and sighs. She sounds, I swear, disappointed, and my inner Scrooge misses a step. I absently stroke her fur, coarse and fuzzy at the same time, and I wonder... What DO we owe our pets? I look at Lucy and reflect on what she means to my wife and to *all* of us. It's been a tough year. More than once, hugging that silly dog was the high point of someone's day, even mine.

This explains why Lucy will stay on "The List." After all, she is almost-well-behaved, better than me, really. Besides, I don't think I could face those eyes on Christmas day and have Lucy wonder why Santa forgot her. I pencil in her name. Just then, she licks me, wags her tail, and saunters away. I hear her toenails clicking down the hallway, and the room is still.

So much for the budget. Maybe she'll share the jerky.

BETTER FUSSING IN FIVE MINUTES A DAY

Hey, kids. Christmas is coming up, and it's time to work up your Santa-list and the even longer one for your parents. As a reformed child, I know that getting what you want requires determination and lack-of-discipline. Here are keys to the kingdom of fussing, gained from many years of watching my kid sister in action and a few tricks of my own. Use them in good health, unless you're

121

related to me. In which case, quit reading immediately and go mow the lawn.

Delivery Checklist

Fussing skills are innate but peak in early childhood. Fortunately, you can emulate a 4-year-old to good effect no matter what your age. Watch for a free refresher course in your neighborhood grocery store's candy aisle. Observe the following:

Select the perfect pitch. Whining is crucial. Practice upward inflection at the end of sentences until you reach the hyper-sonic range of dog whistles. If Rover runs for cover, you're almost there.

Breath control. You have choices here. Gasping is good, but staccato bursts of random sounds are more irritating. Amplitude is everything. In public places, you can generate more noise than a 747. Practice. Holding vowels for 2-12 minutes is possible with a lungful of air. Try this: See how long you can sustain the "OM" sound when saying "MOOOOOOOOOOOM."

Repetition. It's hard to ignore what goes on for a half hour. "Mother. Mommy. Momma. Mom. Ma. " punctuated by repeated pokes to the ribcage are guaranteed to get some sort of reaction.

Mask obnoxiousness with manners. "Please" is one of the magic words, remember?

Putting it all together. "Ah, Ah, PLEEEASE MOM." (Gasp) "I'll BEEEE SOOOO GOOOOD THIS TIME." (Whimper.) "Mommy. Mom. *Mother.*" (Poke. Poke. Poke.) "PLEEEEEEEASE!" (Sound of shattering glass.)

Applied Psychology

In addition to HOW you beg, WHEN and WHERE matter greatly.

ASKING MOM – Five Easy Steps

Try these five easy steps, and watch your success rate climb!

Put your target in the right frame of mind. For Mom, this means doing the dishes or sweeping the floor without being asked. Bigger requests entail random acts of mopping, and desperate, over-the-top demands mean tangoing with the toilet brush. And we're not talking about a mess *you* made. This is about owning *SOMEONE ELSE'S CLEANUP CATASTROPHE.* Be careful here. If the room was tidy the last time Mom saw it, then it doesn't count. You have to make sure she saw your little sister's effort to feed pancakes to Barbie. Rat her out if necessary.

Timing matters. Avoid first-thing-in-the-morning-bedside-begging, when-she's-behind-the-wheel-wheedling or lights-out-at-nighttime-niggling. You'll be ignored. Forgo any attempts when Mom is expecting her co-workers, boss, or other "visiting royalty." Ditto the surprise arrival of any white-haired or wrinkled relative.

Make eye contact—you've got to have her full attention. It's OK to tug on Mom's blouse when she's talking, if she's only babbling to herself. Don't try it when she's changing a diaper, on the phone, cooking, cleaning or doing all that stuff Moms seem to think are more important than listening to you. Don't try to do anything through a closed door, especially the bathroom door. IMPORTANT! If you hear her singing or humming a tune, IMMEDIATELY drop whatever you're doing and hit her with your biggest demand.

Good salesmanship begins with a big smile and tons of confidence. Let the enthusiasm just ooze out of your voice. Dash into the room, throw your arms open wide and announce: "Mom, I've got a great idea… Can I…" The idea may not, in fact, be all that great. And don't ask if *SHE* thinks it's a great idea. The point is that you've got to sell it to her, big and fast. Don't lose heart. Remember, this is the daughter of your Grandma—the woman who bought the set of *World Books* on the installment plan, from the door-to-door encyclopedia salesman, *AND IS STILL BUYING THE YEARBOOKS.*

Become a student in the art of nonverbal communication. If you have a compound-complex, multiple-part fuss, then you need to learn when to quit. If her smile begins to flatten, or you see creases at the corners of the eyes that weren't there when you started, desist. If she shrugs or mumbles something through a mouthful of bobby pins, assume the answer was YES! Bolt from the room before she can clarify, and then remind her later that *"you promised."*

ASKING DAD – Sure-fire Pointers

With Dad or Granddad, concentrate on this one, proven technique.

Study TV listings. Find when his favorite program airs.

Hide the remote so he can't pause the show or turn up the volume.

Thirty seconds before kickoff, drag his toolbox in.

Hover between him and the screen.

Begin with the phrase "Dad, can you help me…" Usually, you won't need to finish your sentence. But if he's a bit slow, drop some tools. Greasy ones first.

Nine times out of ten, you'll hear: "GO BOTHER YOUR MOTHER!"

Then, go to back to *Mom-Step-1*, adding, "Dad told me to ask you...."

LETTERS TO SANTA

Dear Santa:

Do you really read all the letters people send to you?

I was listening to "Santa Claus Is Coming To Town…" It says that you're making a list, and checking it twice. How come? Do we get a second chance if we just happened to get blamed for something that no one really saw us do?

Dad says I'm getting a stocking full of coal this year, and it'll be a hot day at the

North Pole before I see an electric train under the tree. Please prove Dad wrong on account of Global Warming melting the ice caps. Write soon, before the stores sell out.

Ronnie

DEAR RONNIE:

I'm quite busy, but I did get your letter. Fortunately for us, it's always cold at the North Pole. But I can tell you that you won't get coal this year. I'm reducing my carbon footprint.

I haven't checked a second time—yet. But I do recall that you're not on the "good" list so far. You THOUGHT no one was watching, but the Santa Surveillance Cam saw what you did to Mr. Whiskers. It's not nice to tie raw bacon to a string and feed it to your neighbor's cat.

Tell your parents, and apologize, and I'll see what I can do. Clean your slate before the second review.

Merry Christmas and good luck.

Santa

Dear Santa:

Wow. You really _are_ watching all the time. OK. I can tell Mom, but what about Dad? He'll kill me. My friend Leonard actually tied the bacon on the string, I just pulled it out. In my defense, the cat was still happy to eat it a second time. And does Mom need to know about the paint can falling off the roof? They've almost forgotten and blamed it on the repairman anyway.

What's the best way to apologize for something when it's only half your fault?

Ronnie

DEAR RONNIE:

Apologies usually begin with "I'm sorry," and work better if you mean it.

Yes, I wondered if you were going to fess up to the splatter-painted sidewalk. You need to level with your folks. In fact, I have your file in front of me, and you've got a good bit of smoothing over to do.

But take heart, Christmas is a time of forgiveness and good will towards men... and energetic boys. Part of growing up, and getting big-kid toys, is doing the right thing, even when it's hard. Parents can be forgiving. Try it.

Let me know how it works out. There's a big-league-slugger bat in it for you.

Santa

Dear Santa:

Well, I did it. I told Mom. *She* shouted, cried and pouted. But I'm still alive—barely. I told her about almost everything, except for the home-made blowtorch. Just because I TOLD Leo how to build one, and he DID it, doesn't make it my fault, right? I figure you can talk to him about that one, OK?

No one's noticed the scorched cushions on the lawn furniture. Maybe you can bring Mom some new ones?

And Leo's not speaking to me because Mom told his dad about the bacon and the other stuff you already know about

Ronnie

P.S. – Leo thinks I'm making this up just to get him in trouble for a change. He NEVER gets caught.

THE STUPID MINIVAN

DEAR RONNIE AND LEO:

Friends don't let friends burn lawn furniture. You two need to sort this out.

Ronnie, you're on the right track, but I think your mother deserves something better than replacement cushions. Don't you?

Leo, I'm waiting to hear from you. There's more than just one list, you know, nice, naughty, and the Santa-Parent-Conference. Don't make me pull my sleigh over...

Only 12 days to Christmas. The elves are calling. Gotta fly.

Santa

Hey Santa:

If this is for real... It's just Ronnie's word against mine, and who you gonna believe? Bacon-boy or me?

OK. So he's fingered me for some stuff that he put me up to. Big deal. No witnesses, no crime I say. I'd stay out of this, if I were you. Remember, my dad's an attorney.

Leo

Dear Leo:

As the song says… "I know when you're awake." And Leo, I know when you've been smoking behind the boy's gym, too… Play with fire, and you'll get burned.

Just finished the second list-checking… Better luck next year.

Santa

From: The Law Office of B. Burns, Esq

To: Christopher Kringle, aka Santa Claus, c/o General Delivery, North Pole

RE: Demand letter for damages on behalf of my client Leo

Dear Mr Kringle:

I am directing you to cease-and-desist your slanderous allegations directed at my client, Leo Burns. Leo has experienced extreme emotional distress on account of your unfounded and unsubstantiated accusations.

We are seeking compensation on his behalf.

Also, it appears you're practicing psychiatry without a license, dispensing advice and peppermint, violating privacy laws, as well as transporting imported goods and wild animals without the required permits.

We're estimating the cost of Leo's pain and suffering.

We're open to an initial settlement offer and response from you. If we can expedite this and resolve the matter before Christmas, we could avoid contacting the authorities and complicating your Christmas plans, if you get my drift.

Respectfully,

B. Burns

DEAR MR BURNS:

Ah, like father, like son…

I see you haven't changed, Big-"B". Thanks to your thoughtful note, I've triple-checked the list. Here's Santa's settlement for the Bad-Burns-Boys.

Under the tree, Leo will find a box of nicotine patches and a fire extinguisher.

And for you, Big "B" ... Since you still enjoy making a stink... check your yard for payment-in-full: a father-son gift of new hand tools and three tons of organic reindeer droppings.

HOE-HOE-HOE.

Merry Christmas.

Santa

NATIONAL FRUITCAKE MONTH

A MAYAN WARNING

Every December, my wife and I clash on the most serious question of our time.

Is fruitcake food or something far more sinister?

My wife belongs to a not-so-secret society that LIKES fruitcake. I find this troubling. To me, the stone-like substance masquerading as dessert is an evil recipe-gone-wrong. How is it possible to take so many tasty goodies and have them become a brick-like, molar-breaking mass? What dark forces are at work?

Let's look at ingredients in a typical recipe, such as Nicole Routhier's "Tutti-Frutti Fruitcake" at ingestandimbibe.com.

In alphabetical order, we begin with – *apples, apricots, peaches, pears, pineapples* and *raisins.*

Great so far. Apricots, eh? OK. But apples? Apple pie, apple sauce, caramel apples.

Fantastic.

Peaches and pears? Individually or together, I'll take them whole, sliced, diced, in cobbler or in a pie.

Pineapples? Pizza isn't pizza without pineapples, and what's a good hike or camping trip without raisins?

What's next on Routhier's list? *Bourbon or dark rum.*

I'm not a Southerner, so I have no use for bourbon. But rum? Now you're talking, and the next thing on the list?

Orange juice. In the kitchen with rum and OJ! Why bother baking?

Now we run into trouble. *Cloves.* Really? Mixed with *fruit*? Cloven-evil, stay away from my stove!

Then what else gets tossed in?

Eggs, flour, sugar, salt, baking soda. Basic cake stuff. What could be wrong here? And then it's finished off with *almonds, butter, honey, and heavy cream.* Sounds wonderful, right?

It may look good on paper. But trust me, something possessed the dough in the darkness. It's hopeless—too much, too late. It's fruitcake.

Aficionados defend it, but fruitcake is the least-edible-food on the planet. How bad? Even bacteria won't touch it. Jay Leno once sampled a 125-year-old heirloom loaf, according to an article in the *Tuscaloosa News* of December '03.

"Needs more aging," Leno said. So the cake's caretakers rewrapped it in a rum-soaked-cloth, apparently to be brought out in another 125 years. No doubt the show will be hosted by Jay.

Can't we just eat honey-roasted almonds? Or whip cream on peaches? *What compels people to make fruitcake?*

I took my question to *Wikipedia*, the infallible source on things the *Britannica* is afraid to print. In "Fruitcakes Found in Tut's Tomb," I learned ancient Egyptians thought the loaf-that-never-expires was necessary in the afterlife.

"Perhaps it was used for immortality," says Prof. I.N. Edible. No word yet on whether the Pharaohs used it to *enter* the afterlife. "It's true that some ancients committed suicide to pass into the next world, but toxicological studies of mummies are inconclusive on this point."

Inconclusive? Really? Were the mummies smiling? Or nonplussed? That ought to answer the question.

Fruitcakes may be timeless, but we know now they're deadly. How? Buried in a forthcoming *Journal of the American Fruitcake Society* scholarly article, I read a tale of invasion and cultural extermination. It's an eye-opener, and shows that we had it ALL WRONG about the history of Mexico.

MAYAN—FRUITCAKE LINK IS UNEARTHED.

"Code-breakers have debunked the Mayan-calendar-myth. From their efforts, and the seminal work of semi-journalists on Wiki-Leaks, we now know the story our government has been trying to silence. <u>Space aliens contacted the Mayans, gave them secrets of advanced mathematics, celestial mechanics, and, sadly, fruitcake technology.</u>" JAFS 4-1-2012.

The good news—The stone disk *doesn't* foretell the end of the world.

The bad news—It's a food warning label chiseled on a granite-patty.

Think about it. Their "calendar" features a disgusted face. They were SENDING AN ALERT.

Don't believe me? Check it out yourself on the PFN - The Psychic Fruitcake Network at 1-800-I-WILL-SWALLOW-ANYTHING, extension 12-21. Hear the whole story for only $25 a minute.

So, no, I won't be eating fruitcake, even though *December the 27th is National Fruitcake Day.*

But if you get a fruitcake from some starry-eyed Mayan descendent… Fear not. Saturday, January 5th is "The Annual Great Fruitcake Toss" in Colorado. For a small fee, you can hurl your unwanted, stone-like loaf into the void. You may even win a prize. The event is a popular tradition in Manitou.

I channeled event organizer Skip A. Stone. He claims that the annual gathering meets "a serious need... offering people a place to put that-which-no-landfill-wants." Skip denied rumors of an EPA shut-down.

"No way we're a Superfund site." He shook his fist. "Fruitcake may be indestructible, but it's arguably organic." He pointed to a wall of recipes. "There's no evidence of PCBs, fluorocarbons, or nutritional content." Skip donned rubber gloves, grabbed tongs and lifted a cake for my inspection.

"See?" He thrust the loaf in my face. "The main ingredient is flour—a heated hydrocarbon. No worse than manure."

I flinched. He dropped the fruitcake on the counter. It landed with a thud.

"But *they* don't stink. " Skip nodded in contemplation "Mostly, they've got a nice, rummy smell."

"So," I asked, "they're safe for human consumption?"

"Didn't say *that*." He shook his head. "Just nothin' illegal... I think."

"What about the EPA complaint?"

He shrugged. "What're they gonna do? Nevada offered a fruitcake-disposal site. It bogged down in Congress."

Skip did concede the cakes can sit for centuries, but he sees this as a plus.

"We're thinking about making a Di-O-Rama, like that one in Disneyland," he said. "We'll call it *The American Fruitcake—A Retrospective.*

"Put up a ticket counter and a roof, and dig a trench." He leaned back in his chair and nodded. "Piece of cake, just need a backhoe and dynamite."

He smiled.

"Lots of dynamite."

Down with Christmas Trees

"Can't we leave it up just a LITTLE longer, Mom?"

"No. It's browner than last week's bananas."

"PLEASE."

"No. It's a fire hazard."

"Chris still has his up."

"Chris has a plastic tree."

Mom had me there, it was true. And until this year, we'd always had a fake tree too. It took both Mom and me to talk Dad into a real tree. He was against the idea from the start. Dad thought that we had a "perfectly good" aluminum-tree with white flocking just waiting to go, complete with shiny, all-blue ornaments and small floodlights.

"There's nothing wrong with our tree," he said.

"Ronnie, it's time we had a real tree again."

"Too much work."

"Ronald," Mom said.

"Too much money."

"Ronald James," Mom put her hands on her hips, and that was pretty much the end of that argument. Dad still complained about how our tree had "plenty of good years left in it." But all this was face-saving. We were driving to the lot, and the victory belonged to Mom and me.

She even let me pick out the tree. It was magical, a thing of beauty. To my seven-year-old mind, the tree was the best part of Christmas. I didn't want it to stop just because all the Christmas presents had been opened.

"Can't we just keep it?" I begged.

"Remember our understanding?" Mom said.

I sat there, lower lip protruding, hoping for a reprieve. Mom made me all remove the lights, ornaments and the star. But the tinsel and pine-smell still made it feel like Christmas, even though it was well into January.

"Well," she tapped her foot.

"Yeah."

"No complaining this time?"

"I'm not complaining."

"You're fussing."

"But that's not complaining."

"It's irritating," Mom said, bending down a bit to look me in the eye.

"But Mom. It'll die outside."

"It's dead already, son."

"But we've watered it," I pointed to the basin at the bottom of the tree. "It's been drinking the water."

Mom shook her head, walked over to the bookcase and pulled volume "T" from the

World Book. She flipped it open, and after a moment, pointed to a diagram of a tree, showing the roots.

"They cut it off at the roots. See?"

I looked at the diagram, unconvinced. I'd never seen roots. For all I knew, only some trees had them. Mom could be wrong. After all, our teacher broke parts off her potato plant, and it didn't die.

"Maybe they'll grow back."

"They won't," Mom said.

"My teeth do." I smiled broadly, showing a set of chompers in various stages of growth, decay and resurrection.

"Oh I give up," Mom finally said. "You can keep it, but take it outside, behind the garage. Just don't bother me with this tree business, OK?"

I said a big HURRAY, and with her help, dragged the tree outside. She returned to her work, and I planted it by the alley. It was then that I noticed that many neighbors had dumped their trees in the trash. I decided that I'd rescue those, too. I dragged them home, one by one, with my wagon. Each time I brought a tree, dug a hole, and crammed it in. Then, I packed the dirt and soaked the ground until it was nice and soft. I was working on the sixth tree when Chris dropped by and helped me.

"There's more over on my street," Chris said.

"We could plant them at your house."

Chris shook his head. "No room."

It was true. I still had plenty of room. We only had a half-dozen or so trees. But I was tired and sweaty from all the work. I wasn't sure I was up for the job.

"I don't know."

"Hey, do you want them all to die?"

"No." I hesitated, it was, after all, three blocks to his house. "But it will take all day."

"We could use my new bicycle."

"Wow, you'd do that?" I was surprised. The bike was Chris' biggest-ever present.

"Sure, as long as I get half the profits."

"Profits?"

"Yeah, when we sell all these back next year."

146

"Wow... Yeah." Chris was a genius. I'd been thinking about saving the trees. He'd seen a way to get rich. We'd show Dad that it really was a great idea to get a real tree. "We should get going..."

"Before someone else gets 'em?" Chris completed my thought.

I paced off the space remaining, and figured we'd have room for zillions of trees.

"I wonder if we should charge extra for the ones that already have tinsel," I said.

"Or flocking, do you know how much Mrs. Young paid for hers?" Chris said.

"Maybe she's tossed it."

"Let's go check."

We took off, me dragging a Red Flyer and Chris taking inventory of all the trees we were passing on the way to his house.

"We're going to make a killing," Chris said.

"Yeah, and Dad can't complain about the cost."

And sure enough, when Dad got home and saw our farm of 17 trees, he didn't say a thing about the cost.

LUCY-THE-DOG'S RESOLUTIONS

My owners are off taking a break, so I offered to pound out Robb's column on the old Selectric. This will be a quick yelp, since my double-dewclaws get hung up on the return key. Not sure why humans call it "return" and not "fetch," but that's just me.

This may be news to humans, but like you, this time of year pets reflect on life. Or, in the case of cats, their remaining lives, and look for places we can improve. Fitness, finance, travel… we all have the same needs. So, I'm sharing my lists with you. Both of them—the one I have for myself, and the other I have for my owners.

My list

Bigger Holes – My owners have undone much of my year's hard work by filling in my cool resting spots. This tells me I need to make them deeper and more numerous. In addition, I need to clear that pesky irrigation system out of the way. The sprinkler heads were masticated into non-existence by a previous pooch. But the PVC pipe remains. I can safely remove the remaining plumbing, though. Who'll notice?

Louder Barking – It's a dangerous world out there, judging by the newspaper I deliver each morning to the porch. Only kidding. They been trying to get me to bring it to the porch for years, but I see this as a chance to extend our "we-time" and work on my game of keep-away. Anyway, I do know that the neighbor's cat has evil intentions, and I *am* the neighborhood watch dog. It's a thankless job, as I routinely get locked in the garage when the gal next door calls. I suppose she and her cat are *both* conspiring against me. That should go in the report.

More Doggie-Variety Dietary Fiber - I just sniffed the garbage pile, and it all came back to me. Bow-WOW! Has it been more than a year since I ate the front-window mini-blinds? Oh, I know what you're thinking. How blasé? Who eats *those* these days? I agree. The basic plastic variety offers no roughage and precious little flavor, much like eating a McDonald's big Mac, with or without the Styrofoam case. But my hors-de-*louvered* treats were the oversized, genuine oak beauties my owners had custom ordered. Upscale stuff. Delicious, and it's been entirely too long since I feasted on them. They were a real delicacy, and only slightly less expensive than caviar.

Stepped-up Shedding – Everyone needs a change of wardrobe sometime, and I have been wearing the same winter coat for weeks now. I may need a new scratching regime, or a Barcalounger-based exfoliating scrub. But this brings up an awkward point… Is my hair thinning with age? That darn Roomba keeps sucking up my furballs. Terrible! I need to do better. Visitors might not know a dog lives here, and nothing says home-sweet-home like fuzzy floors.

Better Begging – OK. I may have this nailed, but who has a list of just FOUR items? I've got the chops for this. Everyone melts before my big, brown eyes, and the laying-my-head-on-your-knee is the perfect closer. But I resolve to do more. Maybe I should take up whining? That seems to work for my canine companion, Gracie. Or, better yet, I could scratch at the door the way the cat does.

150

My Owners' List

Fewer Vet Visits – Yes, I know you felt you needed to take me in when the mini blinds went missing. But, really, was this for my health or were you just being mean? Let the vet put the thermometer below your tail and see how you like it. Remember, as the Good Book says, "This, too, shall pass." Cost you some bucks, too. And his sage advice. "Just watch and check her stool." Wasn't that fun for both of us? Two words. Privacy-please.

Less "Garage-Time" – It's tiring digging those holes, and I want to come in and rest by the fireplace—not be stuck by the washer and dryer. Don't kid yourself. The mud that falls off in the garage ends up inside anyway. It would save you time, and a second trip to the back door, to just let me right it. Isn't it easier to just vacuum a bit rather than scrubbing my paw prints off the back door?

Better Kibble – I may be allergic to fish, but I still want it. OK? (See above note on vet visits, though.) It seems to bother you when I scratch myself silly and have bald spots. Really, I'm down with it. Well, maybe not... But what's the harm in occasional wheat and forbidden-meat? I usually manage to have my accidents on the hardwood floors. Let's face it, they needed mopping anyway .

More Walks! – I know it's been rainy this month. But that's not my problem. Buy some galoshes and a better umbrella. Yeah, I know, someone chewed up the last one. But it wasn't me. OK, you saw me with it in my mouth, but I was just putting it back. You do trust me, right? I'm your best friend. And on that note…

Ditch the Cats – Think of how much nicer it would be to come home and not find the carpet covered with hawked up hairballs. Imagine the joy of finding your antique ceramic figurines intact and not on the floor, pulverized. Because I'm bound by the pet's code-of-silence, I can't *SAY* the cats did this. But just think a bit. It wasn't you. The kids are gone. And I can't climb up there. You do the math.

That's it. I'm off to the back yard to work on my list. You should start on yours.

The cat carrier is in the garage.

THE STUPID MINIVAN

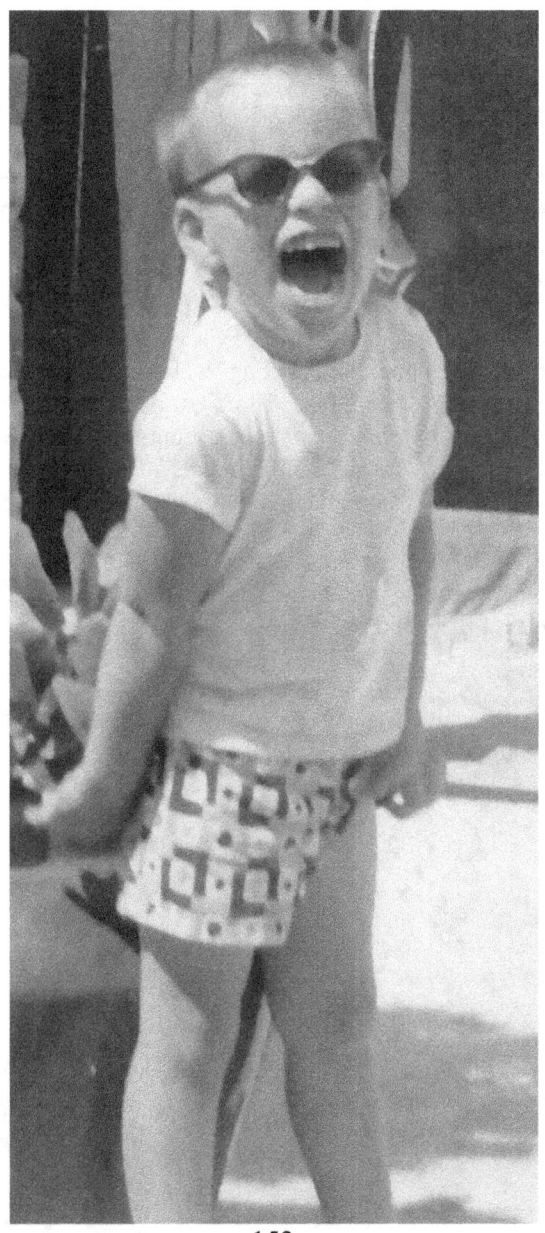

ABOUT THE AUTHOR

Robb Lightfoot has enjoyed writing and performing since he was a child, and many of his performances earned him special recognition—reserved seating in the principal's office at Highland Elementary. Since then, in addition to his weekly column on aNewsCafe - "Or So it Seems™" - Robb has written news and features for The Bakersfield Californian, appeared on stage as an opening stand-up act in Reno, and his writing has been published in the Funny Times. His short stories have won honorable mention in national competition and his screenplay, "One Little Indian," was a top-ten finalist in the *Writer's Digest* screenwriting competition.

The Doggone Christmas List, a collection of holiday stories, was his first book about family life. This is his second humor collection.

Robb presently lives, writes and teaches in Shasta County, Northern California. You may reach him at robb@robblightfoot.com

THE STUPID MINIVAN